NOT CROSS
CRIME SCENE DO NOT CROS
CRIME SCENE
Murderously
Yours

TOPIC CONTENTS

Serial Nos	Chapter Name	Page Nos
1.	Introduction	03
2.	Dedication	04
3.	Copyright page	05
4.	Author's legal disclaimer	06
5.	Chapter One – *The criminal & the cripple.*	07
6.	Chapter Two - *Strange bed partners.*	54
7.	Chapter Three – *Nothing lasts forever, not even love.*	79
8.	Chapter Four – *The "killer" or "kill her" bathroom.*	85
9.	Chapter Five – *The love of money is the root of all evil.*	91
10.	Chapter Six – *Maid in heaven.*	105
11.	Chapter Seven – *The Portuguese Chapel.*	127
12.	Chapter Eight – *Debacle in Sharjah.*	136
13.	Chapter Nine – *Accidental Drowning.*	139
14.	Chapter Ten – *Death never pays, Insurance does.*	147
15.	Chapter Eleven – *Time heals wounds or Time buries wounds.*	150
16.	Chapter Twelve – *Everything that has a beginning has to have an end.*	153
17.	Synopsis	Back Cover

INTRODUCTION

Denzil Dias

In 2024, and in any part of the globe, modern day parents today shudder at the thought of their loving children experiencing the most dangerous and natural drug in the world. The drug called, love.

Having fallen in and out of love multiple times, every parent knows the thrill, trauma, temptations and troubles that come along with this drug.

Parents tremble at the thought of their children falling, especially falling in love. Because most of the time this emotional falling, to hurts, and leaves life long scars and takes a life time of healing, until they find genuine true love.

This novel, "Murderously Yours" will take the reader on this perilous journey of how even mature and adult people too become childlike, when they hear the magical three words, "I love you".

This novel portrays, that where there is love, there has to be lust. Love cannot survive on its own. Lust can. Lust does not need love and always lust lasts longer than love.

Love is truly, ethereal. The Bible epitomises that Love never fails. But in reality, love fails first, fails fast and fails frequently. Inspired by real life incidents, accidents and experiences of lovers, the novel endeavors to show how fast love can change to hate.

Thou shall live. Thou shall love. Thou shall lust. Thou shall never Murder.

From lovingly yours to murderously yours.

Dedication Page

"Love never fails" - 1 Corinthians 13:8

This novel is devoted & dedicated to all those who genuinely believe in the most powerful drug in this world. **The drug called, love.**

This edition will be available in paperback, and in e book too.

This is purely a "Fiction" book. First Edition, published in 2024 by Inked 2 Write

Book Category: Fiction (Murder, Mysteries, Thriller)

ISBN Number (Paperback): 978-93-341-4146-7

Original cover page artwork and back page design by: Denzil Dias

AUTHOR'S LEGAL DISCLAIMER:

This, "Murderously Yours" Novel is a pure work of fiction. Names, characters, businesses, organizations, places, events, incidents and accidents, either are the product of the author's imagination or are used fictitiously. Any resemblance to actual persons, living or dead, events or locales, is entirely coincidental.

This book comes under the fictional novels category, under the genre of murder and thriller mysteries. All incidents, dialogues, and characters, are the products of the author's and writer's imagination and are never meant to be construed as real.

Freedom of expression is a fundamental human right, and a central tenet of any fictional author's work and livelihood.

If any real-life historical persons, whether alive or dead, appear to be similar to any of the characters of the novel, then this is purely incidental, accidental or coincidental by nature. They are entirely fictional characterizations and are not intended to depict any real-life persons or actual events whatsoever.

The purpose of the book, like the Millions of Bollywood fictional movies made on myriads of topics, is purely for entertainment.

The ideas, comments and opinions of the fictional characters are part and parcel of the central story line and are not meant to hurt, insult, or desecrate any individuals, societies, or organizations names.

Fiction can never become Fact and Fact cannot become Fiction. It is imagination that is deadlier than the reality.

If for whatever reasons, you the reader find the contents of this novel, disgusting, disparaging, distasteful, deceitful and damaging to your reading tastes and sensibilities, then immediately drop the book in a trash can.

Chapter 1

The Criminal and the Cripple.

Today, I am going down memory lanes, to recall and recollect a true story of deep love, deeper lust and how the four-letter beautiful word of love can easily turn into vengeful hate. Once I conclude my story, only you can decide, what really is the truth and cautiously shift fact from fiction.

Similar to the city of Las Vegas saying, that whatever happens in Las Vegas stays in Las Vegas. In like manner, whatever happened in Goa, stays dead in Goa.

This story begins in an idyllic rural village of Loliem in extreme South Goa. Perfectly sandwiched between the border hinterland villages of South Goa and the rural villages of Karnataka state in Southern India.

Anand Ashram (Ashram of Joy) was very true to its name, a very joyful place for tourists and solace seekers from India and abroad too. It was one of those reclusive resorts where authors and writers loved to get lost in time, digging deep into their recesses of their mind for their next bestseller story.

Most of the Goan locals who settled inside and around the ashram were mostly retired people, tired from the daily grind of responsibilities and of raising families.

Now in their last lap of life, they rightfully deserved to treat themselves to some luxury called quiet and peace away from the wild parties and crowds of Palolem beach.

I purchased a decent beach bungalow on the quietest and farthest side of Pollem beach. This beach is the first beach of Goa, if you are entering by vehicle from the Karwar highway road.

If you are visiting from the upscale touristy areas of North Goa then Pollem beach happens to be the last beach that one can say bye while crossing the interstate borders of Goa.

I was used to commuting daily between the commercial South Goa city of Margao and Canacona. Both cities were separated by the ever-green winding ghats of the Western Sahyadri's having a short motorable distance of around 35 kms.

I ran a Luxury Toilet and Bathroom accessories and fittings shop in the heart of Margao city. I was generally busy and occupied daily with early morning customers from 10 AM till 01 PM in the early afternoon. The afternoons in Goa for shopkeepers was for the Susegad (noon nap) Siesta. The evening, not so busy session was handled by the shop staff. My afternoons and evenings were kept free for house visits, for site visits and on-site consultation with clients.

I always worked the American style, five days a week, having Saturday and Sunday totally free for my fun, frolic and frivolity. Otherwise, what was the use of working in Goa, if you could not party and holiday at the same time.

Over the weekends, sometimes I used to visit my old-time acquaintance turned friend, CID Officer Achut Pednekar. We became friends over my repeated visits to his office for Passport and Visa issues every year. As I was an NRI settled down in Goa. I called him AP in short. We were used to having his favourite spirit, DSP or Director's Special whisky.

Interesting in India, majority of the IMFL (Indian Made Foreign Liquor) have brand names such as Director's Special, Officer's Choice, Wild Tiger, Old Monk, Kamasutra, and many more.

Achut Pednekar plays and important role in this true story of mine. A little information about Achut at the beginning won't do much harm. He has been working all of his life in the Police Department of Goa. Over the years, he proved his forte to be within the FRO office.

In present modern days' time the FRO stands for Foreigners Registration Office. Earlier a couple of decades ago, it was humorously named as ARO for Aliens Registration Office, NRI's like me and other white skinned foreigners being tagged as aliens in India.

Achut Pednekar from the IAS (Indian Administrative Services) cadre was nearing the end of his fruitful career and was soon going to get retired in a couple of years' time. Most of the long staying foreigners on tourist and business visa always had some problem-solving work with this officer and he was always there to serve you, if you kept him happy in return.

Achut with his tall height, large frame body with broad shoulders and a very large pot belly filled will all types of Goa beers, without his official uniform looked more like a pimp and much less than any physically active police officer.

Another important person, I need to introduce to you right at the forefront is Dr. Tony. That was his short name from his full name of Anthony.

Achut was busy keeping tourists inside the frame of foreign visa laws, while Dr. Tony was practicing his Drug therapy and medicines on tourists who were bound on visiting the seven heavens and back in Goa.

Dr. Tony had his huge hospital setup situated at the world famous Calangute beach village. He was available on appointments only on the weekends of Saturday and Sunday at his Life Clinic at Colva beach city.

Other than drug rehabilitation therapies, which raked in most of the money for the doctor, he also attended to general emergencies and pregnancy cases.

What is Calangute beach to North Goa was Colva beach so to South Goa. Colva is the most crowded and most visited beach by tourists staying anywhere close to Margao city.

Doctor Tony's hands were always full with overflowing patients. He not only had the gift of the gab, but also had a certain healing touch, that made many far-flung patients his first favourite doctor.

He always used to jokingly tell his patients, that if he did not take a regular restful break from his work, then he too would fall sick.

Over the weekends, Doc Tony loved to play and gamble over a game of serious chess. Somehow the local Goans were not so good at chess, which Doctor Tony used to always whine about.

But when he found a challenging mate, then all he wanted was to sip over his Cashew feni and keep staring at the Chess board to make his next move.

Even while practicing his medicine over the weekends at Colva, Doctor Tony made sure that he was not very far away from his chess board and his wooden chest full of feni bottles.

Doctor Tony and Achut were dear friends due to their professional line of work. Whenever the tourists and foreigners had legal problems with passports and visas, they would visit Achut and if they complained of over consumption of drugs or drug related problems, then Achut would recommend Dr. Tony.

Every weekend over a game of chess, both the doctor and the police officer would squabble over amounts of commissions that the doctor owed him, for Achut providing him customers regularly. Every patient was another customer. Nothing more than that to both of them.

On one hot summer morning of May, I was busy packing and picking up all the accessories associated with a certain model of Ceramic Bath tub, before getting loaded on my Mini Truck.

After putting all the fittings and fixtures and the tub, while passing by Margao police station, I dropped in to say a hello to Achut Pednekar in his city police office.

We had a drink together and discussed the daily local happenings. We were having Hot Nescafe Coffee. As Achut always said, "Hot Coffee at office and Hot Whisky before going home, makes my wife look hot and sexy."

I always felt it best not to comment and add anything on that.

Before leaving, Achut suggested me a lead of an upcoming large-scale resort near Cavellossim beach called as "White Pearl Sands".

I promised him to pay a casual visit to that hotel property site next week. *"If you're going up to White Pearl Sands, son,' Achut said, leaning back in his majestic office chair, 'there's a chance for some new business for you."*

"*Also, there are lots of individual premium villas sprouting up with lots of couples and retired families who have the moolah to blow on your luxurious bathroom interiors. Don't you forget my commission too."*

"Everyone at Cavellossim village, are talking about some sad story of a newly married Bollywood couple who met with some accident somewhere and they came out both alive; but the husband became a permanently handicap. He moves around in his mechanical cum electric chair."

Some Orthopaedic doctor had suggested him some radical robotic surgery and claims that, with long term rest and relaxation the cripple should be able to walk again soon someday.

Achut reminded me that the family of the cripple may need some special bathroom fittings and accessories that could be accessible from the patient's wheelchair level.

'I'll call on him,' I said, taking out my reminder book. *'Do you know his name?' 'Bharat Kumar.'* Achut answered back.

A handicapped man living in a wheel chair seemed to me to be a natural customer for multiple accessories, fixtures and fittings, that met the special needs of handicapped people's new waist length height.

As soon as I had installed the latest waterfall shower, and a bathtub at another location, I had just sold to one of my customers, I drove over to White Pearl Sands Resort on my way back home to Canacona. It was a wee bit diversion, as Cavellossim village was more on the coastal beach road. I had been up there a couple of years back and recalled and had faint recollections of the place as a luxurious rural village of Goa, with a magnificent view of the rolling western hills, a carpet of green fields as far as the eye could see and bang opposite was the sea in the far distance. The salty whiff in the air, made you realize that the beach was not very far away.

That Friday evening, before heading for my weekend by the beach, I decided to pay a visit to Achut's lead while it was still hot enough to convert into a sale.

I pushed my hand into my denim jeans pocket to pull out the tiny handwritten note having the address of the handicapped person. After the boat shaped restaurant, he suggested to take the first narrow dirt path off the tar road till I reached a ramshackle broken-down wooden gate.

There was surely a gate. But it was more broken than built. I got down off my Mini Truck to push open the gate. After some budging it went back, till I had to park a stone to hold it into place. Then I slowly drove around some wild mangrove bushes, till the duplex beach bungalow came into clear view.

There were two vehicles parked in the muddy area. I assumed that one must be of the handicapped husband and one of his wives. I parked my mini truck exactly parallel and in line with the other two.

Suddenly, I heard a man barking wildly loud, telling me to park my truck on the other side.

On turning back and looking at his demeanour, he meant business and I had no other thoughts otherwise. So, I very obediently listened to him and parked my vehicle on the other side of the two cars.

As smooth as a child on wheels, this middle-aged man swiftly rolled himself down the wheel chair ramp and within few seconds he was besides my feet. Before I could exit and get out of my truck, he was there besides me. A Portuguese Cigar pinched between his lips; his muscular jaw reminded mere more of a criminal than a cripple.

He was sufficiently tall enough for even while sitting in his wheelchair he offered me a handshake greeting. His wheel chair was battery operated and with a little push on the joy stick handle, he could move everywhere comfortably around the house.

I was about to push the handicapped person, above the ramp, when he refused curtly and then I noticed him immediately engaging his chair to a stair climber for wheel chairs.

These gadgets come pretty expensive as they are made in small numbers for a select few of the general population. This device is designed to transport people in wheelchairs up and down stairs. It has a motor and climbing legs, and the user's wheelchair attaches to the stair climber with a bracket.

Once off the ramp, he immediately addressed me asking, *"Aap ka subh naam, kya hai? In pure Hindi, meaning, what is your good name?"* looking directly into my eyes. There was this deep abyss like depth in his eyes, of one who has suffered a lot. These eyes were peering deep into mine. *"My name is Suman Pandey",* I replied curtly.

"What do you want? I hope you are not a door-to-door salesman? I allowed you in, only after seeing you alighting from that expensive Mini Truck of yours. What do you exactly want?"

"If I am not mistaken, you happen to know Achut the Emigrations CID officer at Margao Police Station.", *"Yes. Of course."* Pat came his reply.

"During your conversations with Sir Achut, you happened to express your worries of having a comfortable stay at your beach bungalow here at Cavellossim."

I dug deep into to my pockets and picked out a deluxe visiting card showcasing my bathroom fixtures, fittings and furnishings business in Goa.

Panda Bathroom Furnishings

Making bathrooms luxurious for the past decade

"Sir, if you need anything or any service, please do let me know?" Having said that, was about to leave and get back to my truck. And he opened his mouth with his cigar in it. *"You came so far all the way, only to give me your Business Visiting Card"* I blurted back. *"Yes Patrao"*.

"Since you have made the effort to come so far, are you able to show me some demo of your products or works?" I excused myself excitedly and rushed down to my parked truck. I strapped around my shoulders, my laptop backpack, my left hand held a white rollable screen and my right hand clutched a tiny projector.

I needed some darkness, so I asked him if we could enter his house as the projector needed a little darker area. He did not mind.

So, we entered the large living hall area. With his permission I closed all the window curtains and now there was sufficient darkness for us to view the projected video.

For the next 10 minutes or so, I was quietly busy connecting the laptop with the projector and setting up the white screen. He was very sharply and intently watching me all along with a keen eye and watchfulness.

Once my demo video of the various clients works that I had done, was clearly projected on the screen, all I had to do was put my mini sound bar on for the audio to play loud enough.

My advertising and marketing video was 5 minutes long, but he definitely seemed engrossed into the contents of my video.

"Are these all of your work projects?" he asked. I replied in the affirmative. He said, *"Impressive"*.

At the end of the demo video, he suggested that this same video could have been shared over the phone, then why all this effort of showcasing in on the projected screen. I curtly replied, *"Bathrooms are large, spacious and luxurious", "I feel a large screen does justice to my work."*

As I was about to pause the demo bathroom video, it continued with a short documentary video about on shore and off shore gambling casinos in Goa.

It was my good blessing that there was a video clip about professional gambling facilities in Goa. I came to know later that the client was deeply interested in such documentaries and movies on the topic of gambling.

He admitted that his most famous James Bond Hollywood movie, was "Casino Royale" as the full movie background was in a Las Vegas Casino. The documentary caught his fancy and he was enjoying viewing it. He propped forward, his face losing all of its sourness and bitterness as he watched at the projected bright screen.

He viewed the full documentary, till the video's end. It lasted a full thirty long minutes. It explained how gambling in Goa was called as Gaming for fun and entertainment purposes only. But the money one won or lost was for real.

"How was the video presentation?" I asked him enquiringly. Now with the curtains wide open and the day sunlight hitting in the room, I could clearly see the crippled man in the wheel chair. I got the uncanny feeling that he was some famous Bollywood personality or celebrity or he looked like someone famous. I could not immediately recognise him, as I was more of a Hollywood movies fan and not of our own country, Bollywood.

"It was surely interesting and impressive and I am sure that you won't be having much products for handicapped people like me". I had to differ with him saying that, *"there is always something to offer for everyone". "Are you looking for something special?"*

"I do miss my special waterfall showers. I dislike having sponge baths or having water being poured on me with a pail".

"Who did you say you were?" he asked. *"Suman Pandey from Panda Bathroom Furnishings"* I said. *"I have my own retail outlet showcasing deluxe and luxurious bathroom furnishings and fixtures."*

"Maybe I should go to one of the big dealers in Panaji," he said meditatively. *"I don't care to deal with a one-man outfit. When I buy something, I buy the best." "That's up to you, Mr Kumar,"* I said, *"but if you want the best, then it has to be handmade."*

"That's something I specialize in. I could build you a Shower Set that would give you deluxe quality plus specialized comfort. It would include a one horse power pump plus a thousand litre water storage reservoir for regular supply of pumped water"

"Mr Panda, I hope you don't mind me calling you that." Blurted Bharat Kumar. *"Absolutely not Patrao"* I replied.

"Please open on your laptop, the international website of www.freedomshowers.com and have a good look at the wheelchair accessible showers along with cubicles that are showcased over there."

"I need something similar designed and built specially for my present wheelchair needs. Just like a walk-in shower, I need a wheelchair drive in bathroom with all the amenities, facilities and features, where I can do all of my bathroom and toilet duties without any other human assistance." "Do you think you can deliver something like that"

"Yes. It can be done."

'How do I know it would be any good?'

'I'm not asking you to take my word for it. I made a shower set along those lines for Mr Harish, the writer, who lives a couple of kilometres from here. You have only to call him and he'll tell you how satisfied he is with it.' Bharat shrugged his shoulders.

'Oh, I'll take your word for it,' he said.

'What would a set like that cost?'

'Depending on the kind of shower cabinet and other associated features and facilities you want,' I said, *I will need to do a detailed study of your needs and requirements and only then I would be able to provide you with an accurate quotation".*

I heard an insignificant sound exactly behind me, and for no cause at all, I had a chilling sensation run down my spine. Without seeing someone, but having such a strong and queer sensation that made a cold feeling crawl up my spine and into the roots of my hair just below my neck.

I turned.

A woman stood in the doorway, and she was looking directly at me.

My first close sight of Sachaladevi is something I'm never likely to forget till I die. Sachaladevi the Bollywood celebrity, actress, the bombshell of Hindi cinema. Here she was standing tall, in blood and flesh in front of me. In my wildest desires, I could never ever expect of ever meeting the dream girl of every man's wildest fantasies.

She was a little above 5 feet 10, barefoot with a full body nude golden sun-tanned skin tone that comes from lazing hours out in the beach sun. Her hair was luscious to say the least. She had such a long lock of hair, that if she let it lose it could safely cover all her god given assets in front. The hair was graceful, glowing and falling all over her body like a glorious waterfall. Her wide lotus - like eyes were big and blue, reminding me instantaneously of the song, 'Blue Spanish Eyes". One flutter of her eyes and any man would be ready to die or kill for her. She was wearing an immaculate white sari with lots of splattered red Polka dots all over. The draped sari showed more of her curvaceous figure rather than hiding and draping behind it. The sari was not covering her, rather it was exposing all of her assets, even more boldly with 6 meters of cloth covering all over it.

Bharat Kumar glanced around and gazed at her, then he said in a smooth, uncaring tone, *'This is my wife.'* He made it sound as if she was of no significance or value. Looking at her, he went on, *"This is Mr Panda oops Pandey."*

"He's the local businessman from Margao city and he handles the cities plumbing needs. He's trying to sell me a Shower set."

What the fuck, did this guy call me in front of his celebrity wife? A plumber. A Plumbing Guy. Really?

This is what he thinks about me the distributor, wholesaler and retail businessperson for luxury and up market bathroom accessories. A Pipe and Spanner handy repair man.

'Isn't that just what you want?' she said. She had one of those low, husky and dusky voices that went with her shape and the wild look in her eyes. *'It could be.'*

He stubbed out his Portuguese cigar, then looked over at me. *'Suppose I don't like the design for this set that you propose to build? What happens then?'*

"It's your wish if you want or don't want it. Mr. Kumar." At the back of my mind, was his Bollywood celebrity wife. Seeing her on screen in reel life was totally different from seeing her off screen in real life. The difference was as much as in a female mannequin and a live woman.

"I will provide you a detailed quotation with complete list of accessories, fittings, fixtures and furnishings for your tentative luxurious bathroom, developed and designed specially only for you and your specific needs. It will be totally tailor – made and there will be no second copy of the same in the whole world"

Mr. Kumar meditated and digested what I had to say and then he replied back, *"You mean to say that my bathroom will be one of a kind and it will be second to none in the whole world"*

"Yes. I replied immediately."

His wife pitched in to my reply, *"However deluxe and luxurious it may be, for my husband in his present condition it is a necessity and need. Also, he needs to pamper himself to a beautiful bathroom."*

She moved her stare towards me, her blue Spanish eyes scanning my full body probingly, along with a tiny hint of a smile.

She passed by me leaving her scent all over me.

She un effortlessly walked as though she was walking on some fashion show ramp. My eyes were sort of hypnotized as she moved out of her beach bungalow, and I kept on watching her till she moved out of my gaze.

Sachaladevi was such a devi. The word devi is a Sanskrit word that means "goddess". It is a gender-specific term for a deity in Hinduism, and is the feminine form of the word deva. She was a perfect sex devi, diva and deva all rolled into one.

I felt an unknown aching pain in my pants. Something was trying to spring to life from its limpness. Unaware, I had hit hard wood in my denim jeans.

The way Sachaladevi moved so graciously, especially the smooth roll of her hips, separating the slice between her butts would make any dead man alive. Any righteous man too would have forgotten his rules. At that moment, exactly as she moved out of my sight, I desired to see her again.

Mr. Kumar said, *"Since my wife suggested, I would like you to make an architectural animation of the bathroom & toilet that you can design and deliver to me. First only present me the design on your laptop, then we will decide it from there."*

With a lot of attention, I had to pull my mind with lots of effort to concentrate on my business and appointment with Mr. Bharat Kumar.

This gave me another opportunity and excuse to meet Mr. Kumar and to again, see his beautiful wife.

"I will get the bathroom prototype designed first, if you like it and approve it, then we can sign a contract to proceed things more seriously."

"I will be needing to come over to your home, to take physical measurements for making the prototype design. Do let me know when I can drop in for the same."

Kumar replied. *"I am a handicapped man. Where can I go? I am always available here at home." "Only phone me before coming."*

Mr. Kumar started reeling his wheelchair outwards toward the veranda, giving me a cue to leave. I left him sitting in his wheelchair on the veranda. His eyes were watching me till the time I sat in my truck and started driving off. I could see him still sitting on the veranda, in my rear screen mirror. This cripple guy made certain, that I left his property for sure.

As I drove my truck back to the tar road, I purposely drove extra slowly, just in case I happened to spot Sachaladevi somewhere. This never ever happened before. I was aching to see her, once more and here I had not even left her property as yet.

My eyes were roving all around, to see her, but she did not show. This devi had incepted her way in my mind. She was on my mind the full morning, afternoon, evening and even as I shut my eye to sleep that night.

The very next day, I went out to Anand Ashram, the first thing in my morning activity. The ashram was always abuzz with activity every morning when it was full of visitors going on a free educational tour, members attending to their shopping needs, and interested enthusiasts like me who keep loitering around. I was hoping to set my eyes on Mrs. Sachaladevi in the hope that she would come to do some shopping needs. I moved around the ashram aimlessly but not without hope. Soon it was lunchtime, and I did not set my eyes on her, so I decided to have something to eat at the Ashram visitor's canteen and move home.

I phoned Bharat Kumar, and took a confirmed appointment for visiting his house on Friday evening. He gladly accepted the date and time for the bathroom layout physical inspection.

Later I looked up for Bharat Kumar on Google and found out that he was a long-time producer within the Hindi film industry. He also after, his marriage to Sachaladevi then got himself involved in the Tamil and Telugu movie industry too.

Bharat Kumar came from a family history totally involved in the Hindi movie making business. Most of his siblings and first cousins, all were either successful actors, artists, producers or directors. Movie making was in the DNA and blood of Mr. Kumar. Just like the famous Kapoor family in Bollywood, Bharat would pride himself to be a part of the "Kumar" family. That reminded me of the Suiting and Shirting materials brand of S Kumar's, advertisement that regularly featured on TV in the late 1980's.

Mr Bharat Kumar, though he had long association with the Hindi Bollywood movie industry, all he could manage to bring home was bread, butter, jam and cheese so to say to the table. He managed to do well. But not sufficiently well to flourish and become a rags to riches story within the industry.

Sachaladevi turned out to be his lady luck. His ladder to success. This is all the information that I could dig out from the internet for now.

Come Friday evening, early at 4 pm at the assigned appointment time, I showed myself at the beach bungalow of Bharat Kumar. As always, he was sitting in his wheelchair on the veranda, a pipe in his mouth this time and a movie magazine in his hands.

After exchanging pleasantries, he told me to find my way on my own towards the ground floor bathroom and toilet.

"You can proceed to start your work, so go in please. I will be out here on the veranda. If you need me, throw a shout please."

"My wife is on the top floor somewhere; she should be coming down anytime. You will need her inputs and instructions. Bathroom is for me, but still, she is the Boss."

The entire bungalow was huge and spacious and filled with knick-knacks that only a millionaire could afford to buy. I put my small briefcase with all of my measuring equipment's on a small table.

The bathroom, I was told earlier, to be found exactly sandwiched between two bedrooms. Each of the bedrooms had their own individual bathrooms. Plus, this was an independently separate bathroom that was equivalent to the space of a 2 BHK apartment area. I was amazed at the space. One could dance naked while having a shower.

The beach bungalow had a circular design with all of the room's doors opening into the central common lobby area, which they called as their living room.

One of the rooms doors was slightly ajar and I could hear some humming sound behind the clatter of utensils. I assumed this must be the kitchen.

At that very moment, the soft humming stops and out comes from the kitchen area, Mrs. Sachaladevi.

"Good evening, Ma'am." I blurted out"

It was always more wonderful to see her in person, than in my imagination of her. For the past few days, since I saw her on my first meeting with her. She was out of sight, but absolutely not out of my mind.

It is said that, imagination is deadlier than reality. But in my case, it was just the opposite. My imagination did not do justice to her wild beauty.

She was more beautiful than the image I had been keeping of her in my mind during the past few days.

Sachaladevi was wearing today casual home clothes, though appearing exorbitantly exclusive. It was a collarless white Tee shirt, with a rubber imprint on the front boldly stating, *"I am the Celebrity of my Life"*. I could not much disagree.

While reading the text on her tee shirt, my eyes involuntarily noticed the two bobbing breasts, suggesting me that she did not wear a bra beneath her tees. Below her waist was a knee long loose flowing denim skirt that hid all of her curvaceous figure.

I suddenly found my heart thumping and I could easily hear the "thump, thump" of my excited heart. I hoped that it was not too loud for Mrs. Sachaladevi to notice it.

"Hi Suman", she said with a gentle casualness with a gentler smile accompanying it.

"Your husband told me to proceed with my work and to find my way to the main independent bathroom" "Could you guide me to it please"?

I had spotted the bathroom on my own, but I feigned ignorance to let her lead me to the bathroom. Her presence would be precious around my sacred place of work.

"Come follow me" she said.

Like an eager and excited dog, waiting to pounce on a fresh piece of bone, I followed her.

While walking to the bathroom, she commented, *"My husband was highly impressed on the video presentation of your works, that you showed him on the projector" "Is there any way, that I could have a look at it too, without disturbing you or my husband?"*

This was a golden opportunity, that I was not looking to happen so fast.

"Yes" I said. *All I would need is your personal mobile phone number and I could share you the video file on what's app or snap chat, depending on which app you are".*

By now she had pushed open the bathroom door and we were both standing inside. She left the door wide ajar and open.

I started surveying the place with my naked eyes. I could feel her eyes scanning my whole body from head to toe.

The bathroom had couple of its own split air conditioners. In the center, was a mini chandelier too. The bathroom was so huge, that one could eat, shit, shave, shower and sleep inside too, without getting out of the bathroom. This was possible because of a Mini Bar and Mini Fridge that I could spot my eyes on. I forgot. Besides eat, shit, shave, shower, one could comfortably have sex too. With this thought in mind, I visualized Bharat Kumar nailing his naked wife on the large powder table while seeing him penetrating her in the large full-size mirror there.

Suddenly breaking my chain of thought, I heard her, *"I hope this venture of yours will be a success."*

"Yes. I will ensure. It surely will". I replied.

"Ma'am, to be sincere, the place is exclusively luxurious, I would not change a thing, if I had to decide."

"Thanks for saying that. As I was fully involved in the designing process along with a professional interior designer." "But I feel that you are forgetting, that my husband is presently in a handicapped state and he is not able to reach most of the taps, faucets and facilities as they were all placed at a normal standing person's height."

I interjected myself. *"This project would involve a lot of restructuring, repairing, renovating and replacing everything to the reach, comfort and convenience from the perspective and position of a wheel chair."*

"Yes, you are absolutely right" said Sachaladevi and *"You can call me Sachaladevi and not Ma'am please."*

I was explaining what could be done to the new bathroom, but I found a bored expression hitting the face of hers and she suddenly walked out leaving me alone with my inspection work in the bathroom.

After few minutes, she came back to tell me, that the servant has served water and some refreshments in the living room area. When you are done with your measurements, please feel free to join.

It took me a healthy 30 minutes more, to complete my measurements of the entire bathroom. At the same time, I took plenty of still photographs and videos of the entire area on my Nikon SLR Camera.

When satisfied that I was done, I moved to the living room. There she was patiently waiting for me while she was viewing some program on her large life size TV Screen.

She bended herself to reach to the remote on the Tee Poy table stand, and I was blessed with a peek a boo of her white boobs. I was right. She was not wearing any bra under her Tee shirt.

I got myself sit, at the opposite end of the huge sofa and plunged myself in its deep recess. The cushioning sort of wrapped itself around my body.

"Feel free to help yourself ". She courteously said. *"You must be hungry and thirsty after all that work in the bathroom"*.

Just like her husband Kumar, Sachaladevi too had eyes that peered and pierced a person's soul. One had to be careful, what one was thinking in the back of the mind, lest the person had mind reading capabilities.

There was a certain whiff of a scent or perfume in the air and I safely assumed that it must be coming from the person of Sachaladevi. I sure knew the difference in the scent of an air freshener and a body perfume. But I could not recognize the scent of the perfume for I was sure it was way out of my budget or buying power.

"Do you need any help?" She asked me.

"I would need to have a look at the Water tank. The main source of water coming into all of your bathrooms."

"Oh okay," she remarked. *"You will have to follow me again."*

She took me to the back entrance of the bungalow. Outside in the green landscaped garden, she pointed to a huge rectangular patch of cemented area, which she said was the main reservoir and water collection tank that is connected to the PWD (Public Works Department) pipeline of the Government of Goa.

Then she led me again inside and then we entered into a small glass cubicle, which turned out to be a private inhouse elevator to lift oneself to the first floor. But I noticed that she pressed the number 2 button on the machine panel. Slowly the ThyssenKrupp Elevator German Engineering marvel moved up silently. We exited from the lift to the terrace area of the bungalow. I could not stop myself from rushing to the edge of the terrace to soak in the views of surrounding greenery. It was an amazing unobstructed view.

"Do you like what you see? She asked enquiringly.

Here was my lucky opportunity to be a little cheeky.

Staring at her body and looking deeply into her eyes, I replied enthusiastically. *"I have not seen anything so beautiful in a very long time."*

She was not stupid, not to understand my cue. But she withheld any reaction from her side.

She started taking a few forward steps and soon we reached to another huge overhead tank that was placed at a much-elevated height on extended pillars. *"We insisted on the Water tank being placed on an extra height above the bungalow, so that the laws of physics will work and we will get uninterrupted pressure while the stored water was flowing down to the bathrooms and toilets."*

"That was a perfect planning and idea". She had a bigger smile on her face. I assumed that it was her idea.

"How does one climb up and get to the tanks for servicing or for cleaning?" I asked her.

"Oh, we forgot to get that done, before we moved in, so we have a removeable metal ladder."

She moved and from somewhere on the terrace, she came back with a single piece aluminium ladder. I volunteered to carry it. But she insisted that it was extremely light and hence it was not much of a hassle.

She carried and placed the aluminium ladder in slanting position leading on the upper incline of the terrace. She asked me to proceed first, so that she could hold on to the ladder and maintain it steady while I was climbing.

She remarked. *"Do you really need to climb up and see the tank up close?"*

"Yes, Sachaladevi", I said. *"The input and output of the water system are very important in every bathroom".*

She suddenly realized that I have a fear of heights. But she did not poke any fun as most other people did. I liked her for that.

I put my hands on the steps and started climbing. Just ten small steps seemed like a hundred for me. But finally, after a little sweat, even though there was a windy breeze on the terrace, I managed with some difficulty to reach on the parapet of tank floor.

Next, she started climbing up the steps. I was holding the ending part of the ladder to ensure that it does not leave the grip of the terrace edge. She was swift on her feet. Half way up, she stopped and looking directly up to me, she asked, *"How is the view from up there?* As I was looking down to her, from my height and vantage point, with the windy breeze, there was no way she could hide her breasts from my view. I suddenly realized that she too knew that. I nervously stammered and spoke. *"It's a perfect view. Never seen such beautiful rolling hills ever before."*

Her eyes examined my face with that well-informed, cool assessment of a woman who knows all about men and how men will naturally and instinctively respond to what she knew I had just seen.

On reaching the top, we took a moment to relax under the shade of the huge rectangular concrete water tank.

This is a man's job to accompany you up here to the tank. But none of my maids will ever agree to climbing so high, so with my handicapped husband in hand, I am forced to do this. Imagine my fans, ever knowing this about me.

She was doing all of the talking. And my heart was doing all of the thumping. I could hear easily the thump-thump of my not so steady heart beats.

Sometimes when I get depressed from my husband's present condition, I do come up over here. It's much quieter here and the height makes the surroundings much prettier.

I was still quiet and then she realized that I was a little breathless. *"Why are you so out of breath?"*

Another opportunity. *"Partly because of my fear of heights and because of you."*

She looked at me and besides the rustling sound of the wind, there was another deafening silence. The sound of silence.

I broke the silence by changing the topic. *"If you don't mind and if it's not too much personal, how did your husband meet with an accident.?"*

After a brief silence, she emotionally burst into speech, saying,

"I know what a terrible life and feeling that my husband is going through. Always being forced to be in sitting position in his wheel chair for the rest of his life."

She then went on to say, *"I am sure that you must be aware that he was an active Bollywood Hindi movie producer for many decades."* I nodded in silent agreement. She continued further, *"I came to know him personally, when he happened to be the producer of one of my hit Hindi movies."*

"We mutually fell in love, not to say on first sight, but on our first movie set, so to say." "But I wish rather than falling in love, now he could stand up for his love."

Her last statement was very confusing and puzzling. What a play of words?

"I wish he could stand up for his love."

Immediately in mind, came the serious thought that, Mr Kumar could not ever stand up in the bedroom to ever make love not only to his wife, but never ever to anyone else too. What a predicament I thought to be in. Was this what Mrs Sachaladevi was referring too or was it just an emotional statement? This thought left etched in my mind forever.

"Though he was the producer and financer for his films, he on the movie sets happened to become a mentor, guide and friend to most of his younger actors." "As an actress, I was too much younger than him when I met him for the very first time in my life."

I did not dare to ask the age difference between Mr. and Mrs Kumar, as it was most obviously visible.

"We individually did sufficiently well in both of our respective careers. He producing movies as a financer. Myself as an actress. It was best, when it was an in-house production. It was like he was investing his money on his story and my performance."

Suddenly as if she woke up from a spell, she blurted, *"Why am I worrying you with my woes?" "You please have a good look at whatever plumbing systems you want to have a look at."*

I preferred to stay silent. I had nothing much to say. I just felt sorry for her. This feeling of pity got communicated to her. That was enough for me.

After doing my necessary inspection of the pipes and plumbing systems installed on the tank, we ventured to move down to the terrace. This time I stepped first and got down cautiously, while she was holding the ladders latter end on the tank platform edge.

On reaching down, after laying down my tools on the terrace floor, I held the aluminium ladders two legs firmly and told her to start coming down.

She moved down the ladder with her back towards me, so she could hold the two sides of the ladder easily. This was the right way to get down for anyone. But it was surely wrong, for a woman wearing a pleated denim skirt that was easily swaying in the breeze at two storey's height.

How could I not look up and see the skirt flying like an open umbrella with the breeze? She too did not make any effort to conceal herself or to tuck the skirt in between her two legs.

On the first day meeting, seeing her in a white sari and now seeing her insides with her skirt flying high, gave me a high.

Two steps down she came and the breeze blew her skirt enough for me to see two tapering legs with graciously muscular thighs, that were worked out in some gym holding two curvaceous butts that were held tightly with some expensive lacy lingerie panties. So, this is what is called Bollywood heaven, I said to myself in my mind.

On the second last step, she suddenly seemed to sway and fall. Was this tripping, intentional or accidental, I will never ever know the truth even till I die.

She swayed towards me falling backwardly. One thing was for sure. If I had not to hold her with my arms, she would have fallen and hurt herself on the terrace slab.

I rushed my left hand to provide her falling back. In splitting few seconds, her full back body was leaning for support on my arms and instinctively I grabbed her and, in the process, while wrapping my arms around her, my left hand had to cup her breasts to lock her body to mine to stop her from falling. This was totally not planned or intentional on my side.

For a few seconds, we were locked together in this safety embrace. My one left arm around her back. My left hand fully cupping and compressing her left breast to reach for the chest rib bones for support.

She clung to me for support and was frozen out of fright and embarrassment for ten or little more seconds. As fast at this all happened, that swiftly she broke free, her cheeks flushed pink with embarrassment, she stood fast on her feet and without saying anything rushed down leaving me all pumped up high on lust and longing to hold her longer.

I collected all my measuring tools and equipment's and without saying any goodbye's to Mrs. Sachaladevi.

I directly headed to see Mr Kumar who was still idling away his time stuck to his wheelchair, looking nonchalantly at the distant horizon, while blowing on his pipe.

I informed Mr. Bharat Kumar, that I completed the bathroom measurements and that I would get back to him with a proposal and quotation to further continue the process.

That night, back at my tiny beach bungalow at Pollem beach, the scene of Mrs. Sachaladevi falling into my arms and me holding her was getting replayed over and over in my brains, sometimes in slow motion. I could still feel her, definitely 40 D size breasts spilling out of my hands.

Her breasts were of the perfect size to my taste. As I would always say, the breast should not be too small, that one man's small hand is sufficient to hold. The breast should not be so big like a water melon, that even a man's two full hands are not sufficient to cup them.

To make the renactment of the above moment even stronger, I went to my bungalow terrace and sat on the open floor staring at my water tank. There in the setting sunlight's shadow, I could visualize her on my terrace. The visualization gave me a strong hard on.

After a couple of pegs of whisky, I decided that this type of thinking is too risky. So, I headed for a cold shower to shatter my heat of the moment.

While fully naked, under the shower, my investigative mind was wondering, did she really fall or did she fake her fall. I could not come to any conclusion. Real or fake fall, the blood and flesh body were real in my arms.

Even as a sufficiently successful businessman, Suman Pandey could not come anywhere close to the financial assets and hundreds of crores in revenue that Mrs. Sachaladevi was valued at. Monetarily speaking, in front of her financial report card and market value, I would be considered a failure and a pauper.

My meandering thoughts, were suddenly disturbed by the incessant ringing of my mobile phone.

I took the call without seeing who the caller was. *"I am sorry, if I have disturbed you calling so late at night"*. I instinctively looked at my wristwatch. It showed 11 minutes to 10 PM nighttime. This voice in my ears could be easily recognized. It was the husky and dusky deep voice of Mrs. Sachaladevi. The sound of her voice made my heart beat faster and naturally it pumped more blood to all the extremities of my body.

Here I was naked, in the process of drying my body with a towel and in the other hand talking to Sachaladevi on the phone. With a hard on.

"It's okay", I said. *"What happened I asked?"* having met her today itself.

"I wanted to meet you." I interrupted her saying, *"I can come over tomorrow during daytime when your husband is up and around"*.

Sachaladevi spoke immediately: *"So, then you don't want me to come over to your place. This is my best time as my husband daily sleeps at 10 pm after taking couple of sleeping pills which keeps him dead in sleep throughout the whole night."*

My legs were trembling and weak and I did not realize that I said, *"Okay, come over."*

At fifteen minutes past 11, I gave up the thought that she is going to come and at that very moment I saw in the distance a pair of headlights heading towards my house.

I rushed in and switched on the parking lawn lights. My heart was racing at high speed as I waited for her car. She drove herself in a BMW Series 7 Car and parked it in my front yard.

On opening her car door, she was immediately apologetic, *"I am so extremely sorry for coming at such a late hour". "But I had to wait till my husband was dead in sleep in his bed"*

I thought to myself. What a choice of words for her husband:

Dead in Sleep. Dead in Bed

"Please do come inside Mrs. Sachaladevi." Saying that, I rushed to put off the parking flash lights, otherwise some pokey neighbour would wonder who came to meet me in a BMW car so late at night.

Sachaladevi was surely not dressed up for any occasion. Seeing her in her shirt and pant night pyjamas, I asked her, if there was any emergency situation.

"The full day, after you left, I was feeling terribly bad, for whatever accidentally happened on the terrace". "I am terribly embarrassed."

"I came to apologize for whatever happened this morning." She said this surprisingly in a very calm and composed manner. *"As a matter of fact, let me tell you very unabashedly and very unashamedly, that I purposefully fell over you. I wanted to be held in man's strong embrace, which I have desired so dreadfully for the past long 5 years."*

Three things happen to a man when in great fear. Eighter, he flees, or gets frozen or fights. Where could I flee and run away from this situation? I was in my own house. How could I fight the overtures of the most beautiful bombshell of an actress? So finally, I froze. She realized it and to break my tension, she asked me for a cigarette.

I reached out to my cigarette pocket to give her a fresh cigarette. But she refused and asked for the one in my mouth. *"All I need is a few long puffs"* she said.

With my shivering hands I shared my half-lit cigarette over to her. She took a few puffs and reclined into an arm chair and forgot about giving back my cigarette over to me.

"Mostly majority of men, the moment they know about my handicapped husband, they start hitting on me on their very first meeting. This did not happen with you. Even after two meetings. I appreciate it the most. I hate men who subjectify women just into an object of pleasure"

As suddenly she appeared on the scene at my house, that suddenly or rather abruptly she got up and said that she better leave and jump back into her bed.

As she stood again, to walk towards the door, there I could see this time inside her pyjamas she was not wearing any lingerie at all. The slice between her big juicy buttocks could be easily seen through her thin synthetic pyjama pants.

"My extreme apologies once again Mr. Suman Pandey. You are an extremely decent guy." "I better be going, before the maid notices me missing."

My mind was racing at the speed of light. What should I do? Should I stop her from going? Should I force herself into another tight embrace?

In a few moments, I was silently walking her to her BMW car. Without any much delay or hesitation, she opened the door, and drove away without saying any byes.

The whole night I could not put myself to sleep. I was thinking over and over again, the chain of events that happened in the last two days.

I beat myself to glory for not being indecent and making a move in seducing her. She was hungry for the physical attention of a man and here I was having weak knees. I cursed myself under my breath for losing such a wonderful opportunity of some physical intimacy with the famous Bollywood actress. No one was going to ever believe my predicament and situation that I was unwillingly in.

That night, as I could not sleep, so I decided to put my pen to use, referring to the ink and pen paper. I preferred the laptop rather than the clickety clack noise of a mechanical typewriter. Also pen and paper writing is only for personal love letters. Throughout the night, I preserved and before daybreak, I had written an original poetry sincerely devoted to, ***"Sachaladevi in a Saree".***

The next day early morning, while having breakfast of 2 half fried eggs, sunny side up, a slice of Chicken bacon and a few wedges of potatoes, I decided to read to myself the final draft of my poem.

Sachaladevi in a Saree.

Saree is an Indian dress, Devine or Devilish by Design

Makes Sachaladevi to STAND OUT in any line.

Saree's drapes bodies of all SHAPES & SIZES

Girls, ladies, woman, it's for all ages

Sachaladevi in a Saree will make any sage go out of his mind.

I neatly hand tuck the Saree on Sachala's Sexy waist, it falls like a graceful waterfall

For all females one size fits all

Respectable is the Saree

So much Sachala, you can show

And yet you cannot be degrading

It covers what you don't want and shows off what you want

Sachala's Saree's house is the BLOUSE

It tucks in her two best assets, above

Sachala can go Sleeveless, Braless, Neckless & Backless TOO

And none of the Traditionalists will BOO

In my imaginative mind, I draped and undraped Sachala in Saree, both in 6 yards and 9 YARDS

The Saree brings out Sachala's feminine hidden beauty from her Goan BACKYARD

Just one long sheet of material covers Sachala's assets, all

Every sari is beautiful, even if left hanging on some shop wall

But when draped on a full-blown woman like Sachala, it makes her look more elegant & taller

Saree is a body-hugging dress,

Wraps around all SHAPES and SIZES and CURVES

Sari is the only unstitched and untailored garment

Does not need, cutting, stitching or shaping

Indian woman adorns a sari OVER a Blouse (top) and Petticoat (Ghaghara)

European woman loves to wear sari with nothing much UNDER

Makes most Indian men go ASUNDER (crazy)

Sachala in a Saree is my ever favourite

Takes longest to dress

And fastest to undress

Some wear Saree to appear BARING, DARING, OR CARING

To me every FAIR & LOVELY Sachaladevi looks in any Sari, ever more ENDEARING

Saree's make me wonder

Does the Saree make Sachaladevi more desirable?

Or the Sachaladevi makes the Saree more beautiful?

I decided to call Sachaladevi and then thankfully remembered her saying, that her husband does not like her receiving many phone calls, hence she always prefers texting, for which she keeps the notifications sound on silent always.

So, I texted her. *"Mrs. Sachaladevi, can I meet you somewhere out today? How about the Coffee Café inside the Anand Ashram? You chose and decide the time convenient to you."*

Without much delay her message came back: *"04:00 PM"* This was the shortest message, that I ever received from any female.

Anand Ashram at 4 pm

About an hour away from the commercial city of Margao in South Goa, situated in the beautiful Sahyadri mountains of the western ghats was the peaceful Anand Ashram.

Anand Ashram's peaceful facilities included 32 private acres near the foot of a forest-covered mountain, overseeing fields cultivated by neighbouring villagers from Goa and Karnataka.

An interesting Kriya Yoga Mandir housed up to 150 people for yoga, meditations, rites, rituals, and healing therapies.

Anand Ashram as a retreat center was established in 2009 by Swami Kriya Nanda, a direct disciple of Paramhansa Yoganand. Yoganand had stressed the need for "world brotherhood colonies", where people with spiritual feelings could live together, ***"demonstrating that simplicity of living plus high thinking leads to the greatest happiness!"*** Swami Kriya Nanda did his greatest to create groups of this kind, and was successful in creating eight of these societies in America and Europe.

I provided Mrs. Sachaladevi via messaging the address and site location of Coffee Café inside the Anand Ashram complex.

The name of the restaurant was as simple as simple could be: "Organic Coffee Café."

I could not believe my eyes. Sharp at 4 pm Mrs. Sachaladevi drives herself in the Café parking lot. There were many other expensive cars of the other HNI (High Net Worth Individuals) around. But her Lamborghini had to stand out. That too in bright and stunning Candy red color.

Entering the café, she scans her eyes around looking for me. She was wearing an exclusive business suit. Maybe she must have told her husband that she is going out to the Ashram for some work and business meeting.

She approached my table with a magnificent smile on her face. The chauvinist in me got into action and I took her coat and placed it on her chair shoulder. Then pulling the wooden chair helped her sink and park her butts into the seat.

She appreciated these little things and thanked me graciously.

She came to the point of the topic and asked me the reason requesting for this casual meeting. Not demandingly but very courteously.

I too came to the point.

"Last night, after you left little before midnight, I could not put myself to sleep at all. I was thinking of you all the time, all the night."

"I wanted to gift you something precious, something original, something not available in the market, let's say something priceless."

"But, since there is nothing that you or your husband cannot buy for you, hence I decided to create something for you."

"What?" She bursted out. *"You wrote a poem for me. You know to write poetries."*

"No. I am not a poet. I never was. But after a couple of meetings, having seen you closely in blood and flesh, I have started emoting poetry."

Sachaladevi continued. *"No man ever has written any original poetry for me. Not in School. Not in College and not in my entire career. No fan of mine has ever written a poetry for me"*

I retorted back. *"Surely, your husband Kumar, before getting handicapped, must have surely written some poetic lines for you? Come on."*

"Since you insist, yes. This is what he ever wrote for me."

"Roses are red, Violets are blue, Honey is sweet but not as sweet as you"

I had a good laugh listening to the chorus lyrics of Bobby Vinton who was the very first person to record the song, "Roses are red, violets are blue", way back in 1962. The original lyrics of this epic song were written jointly by two song writers; Al Byron and Paul Evans.

Sir Jim Reeves, made the classic hit, ever more popular world-wide, when he resung the same song in his disarming melancholy voice. Jim Reeves sang his version of this song in 1963, which was released on his album, "Gentleman Jim".

The phrase, "Roses are red, violets are blue," originated from the poem,

"The Faerie Queene by Sir Edmund Spenser in 1590. A similar rhyme was published in 1784 in Gammer Gurton's Garland, an English Nursery Rhyme collection.

"Pandeyji, you are first man, who has not pounced upon me knowing that my husband is handicapped and incapable of performing his marriage duties."

"A dear female friend of mine used to always say: *All men are just like dogs. When they see another new bone, they just want to pounce on it"*

"I am very glad to find out that you are not one of the million men out there, but you are one in a million." "You are a rare find." She lifted her glass of wine and gave cheers to friendship and love.

"Can I have now, what is mine?" Befuddled I asked her what. *"The poetry. The poetry that you wrote for me"*

I had scribbled the last and final draft on a full scape paper of A4 size paper. I dug my fingers deep into my front jeans denim pants and pulled out the folded page, having the written poem.

"Sorry" I said. *"For not using some special deluxe paper. I made do with whatever I had on my writing table, last night." "But the poetry is special."*

She slowly unfolded the paper, so cautiously as it were something fragile and breakable. She started reading silently in her mind. Slowly the seconds passed. Then the minutes. I understood that she was reading and re reading it all over again. I maintained pitch drop silence. And then suddenly the flood of tears began.

With the poetry paper, still open in her hand, she moved her crying eyes towards me and asked me once again for confirmation. *"Is this truly original? Is this not copy pasted from the internet? Have you really written this on your own?"* So many Questions.

My answer to all of her questions was a strong. ***"YES"***

She was so embarrassed that she broke into tears, that she excused herself to go to the rest room and freshen up.

Seconds seemed like minutes. Minutes seemed like hours. And then she finally emerged after wiping away her tears and putting on some make up. This was normal for her being a celebrity woman.

Sachaladevi starts by saying: *"Till today, all of the men that have wooed me had wasted no time in physically misbehaving with me or endearing me only for my money. I like it that you are sufficiently financially successful."*

"Up until now, I have not met any normal decent attractive man, who was in control of his feelings and desires. For me, "Control" is a very powerful feature in a man. A man in control can do anything in life. He can achieve anything he desires in life."

"But there is streak of something different in you".

"Three times you got ample opportunity to hit on me. Hit you did. But with this beautiful piece of poetry.

I had to say something, So I said this: *"Mrs. Sachaladevi. I am sure your husband must be loving you very much. After all, your love story was one of the famous Bollywood love stories in the industry."*

She said in an angry tone. *"Please, I beg you not to call me as Mrs. Sachaladevi. It stinks of slavery."*

"Loves me. Bull shit. All he loves is money. He married me for my money. Can you believe it? No one does too.

How can an actress make more money than a movie producer? After all a movie producer is like an investor. Right?"

Now she was asking self – questions and she was self – answering them too.

All I had to do was give her a listening ear nodding here and there to show her that I am truly paying attention to her sob story.

'There is always the possibility that you may happen to fall in love with another man,' I said, *'no one could blame you for leaving your husband. You're so young. In fact, as you, yourself admitted that he is 10 years older than you. He can't expect you to remain tied to him for the rest of his days crippling yourself too. This would make, 2 cripples. It would be throwing your life away.' 'Don't you think so?*

"But when I married him, I took serious and sincere marriage vows that I will stick with him faithfully for better or for worse and until death do us apart."

"Divorcing and leaving him now would be totally easy as any judge in a court of law would on compassionate grounds set me free as he is not able and capable humanly to fulfil his marital and conjugal duties."

"But divorcing him, would tantamount to me as betraying him totally. As by divorcing him I would be absolving my duties and responsibilities of not being even a caretaker during his handicapped days".

Then comes the bombshell of a revelation.

"I totally blame myself for his accident. It was my carelessness that led to the accident of both of us. I was genuinely responsible for the accident that handicapped him. It was I who made him a cripple."

"WHAT"? "What are you trying to say Sachala? By now I had unwittingly and unconsciously dropped off her devi ending name. I preferred Sachala more to Sachaladevi and she did not mind it too.

"I don't think that you were responsible. You are just feeling guilty and beating yourself into misery".

Sachala was wearing one of the finest body-hugging dresses, that any tailor could stich for a good figured woman.

Crossing her long, slim legs under her expensive exotic black dress, she remarked: *"Can I speak to you frankly and forthrightly without any fear of judgement? Can I tell you in detail about the incident and accident that led to my husband's handicap?"*

"Yes, please do feel free. I am all ears to you."

"Bharat Kumar and myself have been married for the past 25 years. Officially married in public legally for the past 25 years. Earlier for over 10 + years, we were in a live in relationship as he did not get his divorce proceedings finalized with his first marriage wife."

"My producer husband has all the possible vices. All the 3 D's and more too. Drinks heavily like a boozard. Experiments with drugs and narcotics at parties. And has Dames too.

He never was faithful to his first wife, who had warned me, but I felt that with my true love and beautiful body I could change him for good. I forgot to tell you about another deadly vice. That is his habit of gambling. Not the conventional gambling in Casinos and Clubs. But a deadlier gambling. He gambles on himself and on his movie stories, which always flop at the box office."

All this time, I was intently listening to Sachala as she was pouring out her woes.

Beyond the Glitz, Glory and Glamour of tinsel town, there was tons of garbage, that was not seen by the media or the millions of fans.

As Sachala was proceeding deeper into the sad story of her life, her tone and her disposition was changing with the contents that she was disclosing to me.

"Twenty years into our not so happy married life, I planned on killing my husband in plain cold murder. I just had enough of him. Enough for a sane person like me to be pushed towards the insane idea of murdering my own husband."

But why kill him, when you can divorce him? I enquire inquisitively.

"Divorce will set him free to destroy another female's life and career. Death will put end to this criminal's life."

I was in total disbelief and disagreement with Sachala. I told her: *"I too have been unfaithful to many a woman or two. That does not make me a criminal." "You are wrong on this."*

Now she had an emotional outburst: *"What the fuck do you know about Bharat Kumar? Before a cripple he has always been a criminal. He is a criminally insane person. He preys like a vulture on weak animals. Just like the vulture is a very patient bird. It waits and waits and waits, till the animal or human cannot retaliate or fight back in self-defence.*

Then the vulture, claws the prey alive, and feasts on its destruction and death. That is the most fit description of my famous Bollywood producer, my dear husband Bharat Kumar."

"Five years back, I found a golden opportunity and I did not lose it. But cruel fate had other plans. Fate supports the evil."

"While on a holiday tour celebrating our 20th marriage anniversary, leaving our two beloved daughters at home, we went on a short trip to Sharjah. After a party, he was totally drunk. This was my golden opportunity. At the airport, there were couple of tall elevators and I was having a drunk and delirious husband to climb on one, while it was moving downwards. I too had consumed a couple of shots of vodka at the party. I very well knew that multiple cameras would be recording the event as it happened. All I had to do was give him a slight "nudge" at the appropriate moment while getting down on the escalator. To keep myself free from being accused of "attempt to murder", I planned on falling down the escalator steps too along with him. I was aware of what I was going to do. He was not. I was in control of my fall. He was not.

I expected him to break his neck or bang his skull to death. But none of that happened. What happened, surprised me all the more. I came out safely with some major bruises and scratches, and he came out of the hospital as a cripple."

"Why are you so silent Pandeyji? *Dar gaye kya. Sholay ka dialogue yaad hai nah. 'Jo dar gaya, samjho woh mar gaya' (One who fears, disappears in death).*

"Sachala, I am seriously digesting your contents. Are you the criminal or your husband is the cripple criminal?"

"Tell me one thing, Sachala. Why so much hate, that you went to the extent of killing your husband, Kumar?" *What is your real motive or intent for killing your husband?*

"With your type of reasoning that way, then half of the worlds betrayed wives would end up killing all of their husbands. Something does not fit. Something does not feel right.

"Wow Pandeyji. You are not just a successful entrepreneur. You have a keen mind for investigation too. I am really impressed with your keen observation."

"Let me get the cat out of the bag. Since I have spilled all my milk in front of you, what's the harm now in breaking the milk bottle? Behind the facet and face of a producer, my husband Bharat Kumar actually was, is and will always be a Pimp. A very professional pimp."

"What the heck are you saying? Sachala. I just cannot believe this at face value. Pardon me for saying that."

"That's not all of it. Wait and see if this shocks you anymore. Around 10 years into our marriage, all was fine, till he delivered a long stretch of over 12 Mega flop movies, one after the other. In some of the movies, I too was the main character or performing artist. It damaged my future as an actress too.

He was borrowing funds from the mafia to invest in his own movies and in the age-old formula story plots of his grandfather's time, which the audience was not loving and lapping at all in the cinema halls. After 12 movies flopping at the box office, one after the other like dominoes, then he found an instant way of writing off his loans with the Mafia by pimping his very beloved wife to wipe off his huge loans. You must have heard of actresses sleeping with the directors for main leading heroine roles. This was not the same. This was much worse. He was prostituting his own wife, so that he could reduce and wipe out his loses and loans. As a loving and dutiful wife, I too naively felt that, genuinely there was no other way. No one would ever know. To cut it short. I finally agreed and succumbed to his repeated requests. I slept my way with all in the mafia and got all my husband's loses and loans cleared until he was totally debt free. YES. WE WERE TOTALLY DEBT FREE."

"You may be wondering; how could I end up doing this shit so regularly and voluntarily. Not really. Over the years, my husband is a controlled drug addict, he slowly and conveniently introduced to me leisure drugs first at home, then took me to the many drug parties that happen regularly in Bollywood circles. Slowly & surely, I had to get addicted. After all, that was my dear hubbys plan all along. Whenever I used to refuse, sleeping with any of his Mafia friends, then he would forcibly make me go "cold turkey" meaning, he ensured that I could not have access to any drugs."

This totally made me ragingly mad. For the first time in my life, I experienced the psychosomatic experience of climbing the walls. I gave in to his requests, slept with whomsoever he commanded, and I got my dose of drugs to keep me sane and back working on the silver screen. Behind the glitz, glory and glamour, no one could see the garbage of Bollywood life."

"I now felt, that my husband, would love me all the more, for having sacrificed whole and soul for him. But what I started getting called was a Whore. That too I ungrudgingly accepted, because that it was what my love for him made me ultimately. The wife a whore and my husband the professional pimp. The money that I made from fucking his clients, gave him a high."

"Still, I forgave him, for it was I who was a fool. It was I who failed myself. Since he was clear of any future debts, I left him to work alone on his projects. I totally refused to act in any of his films evermore. This totally enraged him. But he could not do anything to make more money. His plots were old and flip-flops. His production company did not deliver even a single hit in one full decade of 10 long years. He was literally breaking bread on my earnings. But still I never ever got the criminal inclination of ever killing him."

"Pandeyji, your silence is very deafening. Your sound of silence is making the loudest noise in my ears." "Now you will slowly lose all attraction in me. Whore that I am."

"This is when I decided to kill him:"

"Pandeyji, without getting into the gory details, I accidentally discovered that since I was growing old and less attractive to most of the men in the mafia industry, always I used to hear my husband being demanded by clients for "Naya Maal" (New Stuff) over his telephonic conversations. To keep it short, I found that my husband, my producer husband Mr. Bharat

Kumar was now tempting and seducing his eldest daughter to prostitute for him."

"This is exactly, when and why, I decided that this piece of shit has to go."

Sachala wiped her second set of tears rolling by. I decided to remain silent. I had absolutely no words to console a human being who went through this kind of shit. I decided to stay and stick along. None of us spoke even a word. We did not need too.

The evening passed by. From the nearby Organic Coffee Café store we walked silently and moved to the next door, Ala – Carte Cuisine restaurant. I expected that Sachala would be hungry after all of the repeated crying that she had gone through. The evening slowly turned into night. We ended up quietly eating a full 5 Course Meal. Because the food was delicious and we both wanted to keep our mouths busy and shut.

A little past 7 pm and she spoke her final words: *"Pandeyji, I need to leave. If you want to gossip about my story do so. I will just end up denying everything as fiction."* Then she graciously got up to leave. I was still stuck and transfixed to the chair after listening to her story. After having paid the bill, I was about to leave. But then I ordered for a bottle of whisky and stayed behind, don't know for what.

♥

Chapter 2

Strange Bed Partners

Strange are the ways of partners. Stranger are people in love. Strangers in love are wary of each other. Strange are the ways of bed partners. Everyone falls in love, but few ever stand for love.

The next day, I was anxious to know how Sachaladevi was? Did she had any problems on reaching her home? I could not stop myself from texting her. Control or no control. I wanted to just text her and say hi to her.

I waited patiently for her to text me the whole of early morning. Then after lunchtime, I could not keep my fingers to myself. I said to myself, that I will just say hi and if she does not respond, then I will totally ignore her for the moment and will not unnecessarily disturb her.

Post having a heavy lunch and attending to the store duties, I finally drove myself home at Pollem beach. After a chilling cold shower, while reclining naked on my bed, thinking of Sachaladevi, I finally dared to text her.

I texted. *"Hi"* and to my shocking surprise, I did not have to wait much at all. As though, she was expecting my message or she too was anxiously waiting for me contact her. She responded back. *"Hi there"*.

She continued texting: *"What took you so long to text me? Were you really so busy, that I was not on your mind at all?*

"You are on my mind, day and night. It's like you have rented out premium space in my heart and mind." I texted back.

"Are you okay with living alone on your own? Don't you feel lonely at times? For the very first time Sachaladevi asked me a personal question.

She continued texting: *"I was expecting a strong and handsome man like you to be taken in marriage.*

I replied back: *"I have been very unlucky in love and lucky in lust. I just did not find an emotionally intelligent woman worthy to become my life partner."*

"Are you a difficult person to please and to live with, for any woman? I answered. *"Maybe. You could say that. My outlook on marriage is that it is too permanent, whereas everything in life is temporary, the most temporary thing being life itself." "Nothing lasts forever. Not even love."*

Sachaladevi texted back: *"One must find true love. To find true love, one has to be vulnerable. Vulnerable to being betrayed, bruised, battered and beaten in love. Only then, may, I repeat you may find true love in the process."*

I texted back: *"That is really deep"*

Suman: *"Sachaladevi, I want to return back your favour."*

Sachaladevi: *"What Favor? I did not understand.*

Suman: *"Yesterday night, you came and visited me late at night. Tonight, I want to come to see you. But only if you permit me to do so. I plead you not to say no."*

Sachaladevi: *"I will have to ensure that my husband takes his sleeping pills on time and goes to sleep at his usual time of 10 pm at night."*

Suman: *"Try to increase his sleeping pill dose by another extra pill, so that he is dead asleep, when I come."*

Sachaladevi: *"I will text you further instructions, once he is asleep at 10 pm. See you soon."*

Suman: *"Looking forward to seeing you soon, dear"*

That day was the longest day of my life. Waiting in expectation is a very painful experience. No pain – No gain, I said to myself.

I wished that I could make time move faster. Finally, it was 10 minutes to 10 pm on my wall clock. Slogged at my work appointments, then when at home in the evening ate a Sandwich, Shat, Showered, Shaved and was hoping to get lucky to get some amazing Sex tonight.

The final 10 minutes was like 10 hours.

Finally heard a what's app message notification bell on my phone. To my extreme delight, it was a message from Sachaladevi.

Sachaladevi: *"Arrive at my place, a little after 11 pm. Park your vehicle on the tar road, sufficiently far away from the direction to my house. Then walk yourself on the mud path, till my house. DO NOT come by car or bike at all. I will ensure leaving the main door ajar. I will put off the safety alarms and the cameras too. Remember to wear a jacket with an overhead hoodie. So that no one recognizes you, just in case if anyone bumps into you while walking the dirt path. Wear sports shoes having a PUF (Poly Utherane Foam) sole. Remove your shoes. Tie both the shoe laces and hang it around your neck. Push the door and head straight for the stairs. Tip toe silently but quickly and I repeat again. Head directly for the stairs. Climb only the steps till the first floor. I always sleep alone in the top bedroom. But I will be waiting for you on the terrace. You need to use and engage the lift from the first floor only. That way, the maid will not hear the starting of the lift from the ground floor, as I will ensure to keep the lift on the first floor after moving up to sleep."*

Suman: *"Your meticulousness and attention to details scare me."*

Sachaladevi: 😇 *"I forgot an important thing. Put your phone on full silent mode or full DND (do not disturb) feature."*

I made myself present on the main tar road outside Sachaladevi's house at Cavellossim a little before 11 pm. I had a safe 10 minutes to reach the beach bungalow on time.

Thank goodness, it happened to be a bright moonlit night. Without needing to put my phone torch light, I could manage walking casually towards her home.

In the far distance, I could hear some stray dogs barking. It was good that Sachaladevi's beach bungalow was in a secluded place not having much neighbours in the immediate surroundings.

As soon as I reached Sachaladevi's bungalow, I got terribly scared. Scared as there was not a single room lit. The entire house was in pitch darkness and the moonlight shining from behind cast an ominous shadow of the house in front.

Standing on the veranda, balancing myself on the rails, standing on each leg, managed to remove both of my shoes with some difficulty. Tied both the shoe laces together and put them around my neck.

At the door, I checked my digital wristwatch and the neon green light said 11.45 pm. I was late by many a few minutes. My heart started throbbing, worried that Sachaladevi may have lost patience and finally locked the door anticipating me not coming.

With a short prayer on my lips, don't know to which deity or God I prayed to. Maybe the Goddess of love, Kamasutra. Rati. The goddess of love associated with the Kamasutra is Rati, the consort of the Hindu god of love, Kamadeva:

Rati is the goddess of love, carnal desire, lust, passion, and sexual pleasure. She is often depicted with Kama in temple sculptures and legends.

I gently pushed the main majestic wooden door. To my utter childlike delight, without any creaking sound, the door moved. I realized it was perfectly left open.

Once inside, I stood for a moment, for my eyes to get adjusted to the dark interiors of the living room. I had been here earlier a few days back. So that helped me a lot. A certain curtain was left wide open. It brought in the moons light directly shining on the concrete stairs. I was sure this was the handiwork of Sachaladevi. She was not only beautiful, but had brilliant brains too.

I tip toed myself like a leopard cat, prodding eagerly forward for his kill or to be killed.

The Elevator was exactly next to the stairs, so on pressing the button, a round light glowed and the doors opened with a small whizzing sound. It was pretty noiseless. German engineering at its best. I entered in, closed the doors and pressed the button numbered 2 on the panel. With a delay of a second or so, the elevator moved and carried me to the next second floor. On opening the door, I was now standing out on the terrace floor.

I was wondering, where the hell is Sachaladevi? My mind all the more wandering. I casually walked myself to the edge of the terrace to soak in the midnight views of the vast blue expanse of the skies. It was bright and clear October night, with a pale hint of the approaching cool winter announcing itself by the breeze.

Then suddenly I heard the crystal-clear sound of a key turning in a keyhole.

It was Sachala ensuring that the lift stayed locked on the terrace floor. Everyone knew her regular habit of spending alone time on the terrace even at odd hours.

Also, there was stairway access only up to the first floor. I noticed this, while I was climbing up tonight, there was no continuity of stairs to the terrace. This surely was the brilliant brainy work of Sachala. She had an uncanny attention to fine details.

There she stood. Standing gracefully tall, all alone. With her back to the stainless-steel doors of the German lift. I walked slowly yet swiftly like a stupid prey so eager to getting devoured by the predator. Only time would tell, who was the predator and who was the prey.

Sachala hailing from the south of India, especially the city of Chennai (earlier Madras) was much shorter in height to me Suman an NRI (Non-Resident Indian) having my ancestral roots from the Northern Himalayan region.

We stood silently staring at each other, totally aware of what was going to happen next.

Then Sachala was about to part her lips and open her mouth to say something. My right-hand middle index finger, instinctively touched her two lips, signing her to zip it up.

I let my index finger stay upright on her two lips. Then I moved my lips and placed them on the other side of my index finger. Now the only barrier between our two lips from getting locked was my finger. We could hear each other's heavy breathing pounding our respective lungs against the frame of our ribs.

I felt a firm hand of Sachala, sluggishly pulling away my index finger away from both of our lips.

It was not just the meeting of two lips. It was the summit of two hearts, two souls, two bodies and the confluence or meeting of two rivers one Mandovi from the south and the majestic Megna river from the north.

Time stood still. We locked lips for a few seconds more and then she disconnected and locked me into a strong full embrace.

Then pushing me away, she walked in her one-piece night gown and started climbing up the aluminium ladder steps that was kept reclining against the loft water tank platform.

I wondered, what this wild woman was up to. But I did not dare to ask and break the rhythm or momentum of our frenzy.

I slowly followed her obediently climbing the stairs a little behind her. Once on reaching the top, I noticed the long length and breadth of the water tank which was in a rectangular shape. The water tank had three separate openings or hatches wide enough for a plumber to enter in and do maintenance or general cleaning.

My attention being distracted, suddenly I realized and noticed Sachala standing close to the middle-opened hatch.

On this bright lit moonlight night, with a carpet of shining stars all around the dark black sky, here was one celebrity star of India, dropping her one-piece nightgown by just a tiny twerk of her two shoulders.

Sachala was standing totally nude, under the open sky. What a panoramic view it was of her naked back. As I was gazing at her naked back, starting from her short neck, and was just about to set my eyes on the valley crack between her butts, it is that time that she took a plunge into the water tank.

I followed to the second middle opening hatch and peeped below inside the water tank. There she was all wet and yet hot. Standing half submerged in water a little above her waist. The sudden jump of hers, created a wave pool in the water tank, with the small waves hitting her two breasts, covering it with water and the receding wave once again exposing her taut nipples.

Sachala waved her hand for me to jump in. I too undressed myself. Kept my jockey underwear and shorts dry on the tank itself, just besides her nightgown. I first sat on the hatch opening and then slowly lowered my full body into the water tank.

Without wasting any time, we both engaged ourselves in a frenzy of love making with the water splashing all around.

The last few words I remembered Sachala speaking were: ***"Pandeyji, remember to write a poetry on this."***

---

*"**Pandeyji,** remember to write a poetry on this."*

Throughout the next week, Sachala visited my beach bungalow at Pollem beach on every alternate night.

She would arrive post 12 pm midnight and leave before the clock striked 3 pm, early morning.

We made lots of unhurried love, unlike our first intimate encounter in the water tank.

I remember having made love to a beautiful woman on a water bed, but this was first for me too. Making out in a water tank.

While making love, we spoke very little and we fucked a lot. Our moments consisted of a lot of desperate and violent love making as we knew that we did not have the whole night to ourselves. We had to make the best of the little time we had in hand.

I suddenly thanked myself for handing over her husband Kumar's bathroom project over to my office team. They were overjoyed to know that, they would get total hands-on experience, to design and develop it. As I was busy thinking about Sachala during the day and making love to her almost every night.

On our third love-making event, at my beach bungalow, I had this regular habit always of screaming out while I was climaxing. *"I am Cuming. I am Cuming. I am Cuming."*

But this time something different happened, which made Sachala very happy and it could be seen by her big broad natural smile of contentment.

After our regular bout of love making, I was about to cum. I felt the painful burning sensation in my balls, that my dams of semen were about to burst.

Simultaneously as I came and ejaculated while I was inside Sachala, I blurted innocently but truly. *"Sachala. I am Cuming. I love you. I love you. I love you."*

Sachala looked up at me, and there was that thing again in her eyes. A look of deep satisfaction. Of a woman totally in control of herself. I did not even realize that I blurted out the threw magical words of, *"I love you"*. Only when Sachala recounted it to me, I was surprised myself.

At the next weekend, we met once again at the same Organic Coffee Café inside Anand Ashram. I liked that the café whether you sat in or outside in the open-air garden, there was always a cool carpet of shade provided by the dense growth of trees all around.

This Saturday at our coffee meet out, Sachala was very quiet, pensive and reclusive. She was not at all chatty as on the other days that we met. I had to ask her, why?

"Sachala, I am finding you extremely quiet today. Its not quite your disposition. What's keeping you so quiet? What's on your mind?"

"Suman, do you really want to know?"

"These are the last and latest thoughts going on in my mind: If only Kumar was dead...... if only he was dead. Then I could be free to live with you as I want to be with you, forever. I can never be free from this criminal cripple, UNTIL HE IS DEAD.*"*

"You would be the first woman in the world to kill her husband just by wishful thinking." Suman said.

"Suman, in his crippling condition, he could be handicapped for another 30 years at least. Doctor gave bad news. There's hope of him recovering after some ground breaking modern robotic surgery & physiotherapy".

Suman wondered out loud, *"Well, then, why waste time wishing he were dead? You are not going to wait for thirty years, are you? You've got to ask him for a divorce!'"*

"Suman, divorce will be a bigger disaster for me financially. In his present handicapped conditions, he will automatically win the sympathy of any marriage court judge. Firstly, all my assets will be equally distributed and divided, irrespective of its mine or his. He hasn't any. He will be most happy to get half of what I have. Plus, instead of the wife getting alimony in normal cases, here the husband will claim alimony for being unable to support himself to meet his daily survival needs."

Divorce is not the answer. *Death is the solution.*

Sachala continued saying that money she had lots and could a lot more easily too. The most expensive and priceless thing for her now at the moment, was her freedom.

"If you have freedom, you can always make more money. But if you don't have freedom, what's the use of the money that you don't have the freedom to use also?"

"Suman, I can give you all the money you can imagine, you already have me. All I want you to give me back is my freedom. Freedom from this cripple, that I hate."

'Suman, please! I'm asking you! What would you do with unimaginable shit loads of money?' I suddenly began to think what I would do with such a sum if it were mine. The thought sent a creepy sensation up my spine."

'If I had that amount of millions in cash that would mean having sufficient capital to expand my business,' I said, 'I could double it in a year or much less. Plus, I would love to open branches in all the major cities of India. I would have a service center for every state covering the whole wide country. I would specialize in hand-made, luxurious bathrooms made to order for the wealthy and super rich. I could make a whale of a lot of money.' Sachala added to that, 'You would love to do that, wouldn't you?

And I would love to be at your side and see you Suman achieve your expanded dreams.'

Suman boldly asked her: *"What do you want me to do Sachala?"*

Sachala said: *"I tried to kill him once. I failed. I cannot try again as all the needles of suspicion would point over to me". "Plan a plot to kill him".*

Suman could not believe his ears.

"Jaan, where are you"? called out Mr. Bharat Kumar to his dear and beloved wife, that early Monday morning.

Sachaladevi on hearing her husband's call, diligently raced to the ground floor veranda.

"What happened?" queried Sachala.

"You need to get organized and prepared for your movie work to be shot at the shopping malls of Sharjah. In connection with that, and in conjunction with the middle east laws, I have booked an appointment with an insurance attorney to meet us both here today."

"I think, you may have forgotten. Your next unnamed movie project is an action-packed violent adventure movie set on the sand dunes of Sharjah."

"UAE (United Arab Emirates) laws require important celebrity actors and actresses to take sufficient insurance towards accidents, eventualities and for risky work environments."

"I did not forget about it. But it was off my mind."

Later that day at Mr. Bharat Kumar's residence.

"Jaan, referring to his wife Sachala, this is Shamsuddin who I was telling you about.' Shamsuddin thrust out his hand. He looked a bit too young, looking fresh and vibrant like just out of college and was bright and as sharp as they come". Sachala shook hands with him. *'Mr Sams,' he said, Shamsuddin loved when anyone called him by his short pet alias name of Sam's.*

Kumar stated: *"I understand from Officer Achut that you look after all the foreign customers from India who are operating some or part of their businesses in the middle east countries.' 'Well, I wouldn't say all of them, but I certainly look after most of them.'* Mr. Shamsuddin said.

Shamsuddin introduced a little about himself and his insurance solicitor company's background:

Sam's shared some his insurance company brochures which read as below. He also reminded that this same information and educational knowledge was freely available on his company website for reading, sharing and downloading for every customers benefit.

Life insurance in UAE supports you in protecting the future of your family and all your beloved ones. If the insured passes away suddenly, the family will be financially protected and get the whole amount.

You may choose the best life insurance in UAE for you and your family's security from among the many insurance law services in UAE that provide life insurance policies in UAE based on their needs and income.

Family Care and Protection

Life insurance UAE is an agreement between an insurance company and a policyholder under which the insurer agrees to pay death benefits to the policyholder's beneficiaries in case of the latter's early passing. A monthly or lump sum premium is paid by the policyholder in return for the security obtained.

With different life insurance alternatives, you may also invest and increase your money at the same time and get a cash value after a certain amount of time.

A UAE insurance policy provides financial assistance to your dependant family members so they may manage difficult circumstances and pay their bills without having to make lifestyle compromises. Beneficiaries may also utilize the cash provided to pay off debts and mortgages.

This is to ensure that your dependents are not responsible for any debts on your behalf.

Protects the family members – After the insured passes away, the family receives financial assistance from the insurance provider depending on the policy's payout.

Guaranteed returns: After the insured person passes away, the insurance firm is required to pay the nominee or insured's family the sum promised amount.

Loan facility – The person may also choose to combine a loan with a certain life insurance policy.

Future savings – Some insurance offers a bonus upon maturity, which aids in future savings.

Coverage for Medical Expenses: Some life insurance plans pay for the hospitalization and treatment of serious illnesses.

Numerous life insurance firms: depending on the customer's demands, life insurance firms in the UAE provide different insurance plans.

Types of Best Life Insurance in Dubai, Abu Dhabi & Sharjah, UAE

The UAE's competitive insurance firms provide a variety of life insurance programs. Although each plan protects your dependent family members, they each have their own distinctive set of benefits and advantages. moreover, Life insurance Sharjah cost depends on many strategies and the level chosen.

Term Life Insurance

Policies for term life insurance only provide insurance coverage for the duration of the policy, which may be one year or longer. If the policyholder dies during the policy term, the death benefit will be paid to the policyholder's family.

As long as the premiums are paid, protection will be provided. Although the policy expires after a specified amount of time, some term insurance policies allow for renewal. For each renewal, premiums frequently increase with age.

Whole Life Insurance

A whole life insurance policy, also known as a straight life insurance policy, is undoubtedly the only UAE insurance policy that provides coverage up to the age of 95. By paying premiums for a limited term, the investor or client can benefit from the whole life insurance policy's protection.

Typically, the whole life insurance coverage has a flat premium. It is an insurance plan with an investing component.

Universal Life Insurance Plans

It allows the policyholder to customize their coverage by including a variety of investment possibilities.

In addition to many other benefits, the insurance offers a death benefit and tax advantages.

Personal accident insurance

Personal accident insurance coverage is an optional insurance option that you can include in your basic life insurance policy. After the policyholder passes away, this insurance policy would help the family of the policyholder with costs like funeral costs and other expenses. This policy has some restrictions.

Indexed Universal Life Insurance

It is usually universal life insurance with a cash value element and flat or rising death payments. On the investment component, the premiums paid for the indexed policy receive fixed or equity interest rates. If the policyholder passes away unexpectedly, the insurer pays the guaranteed death benefit, which includes any incentives that have accumulated over time. The cash value is given to the policyholder as a bonus when the insurance expires.

How do life insurance policies work in the UAE?

The policyholder pays a monthly payment to the insurer in exchange for monthly coverage.

In the event of death or other major threats, the insurer guarantees the agreement for the family of the insured's financial security.

When the agreement matures, the insured receives a maturity benefit. Depending on the type of coverage, this may vary.

Why Life Insurance in UAE is very important?

According to UAE health insurance law, life insurance in Dubai, Abu Dhabi & Sharjah provides you with a number of additional advantages, including choices for investing, protection against catastrophic sickness, financial development, and more.

The following are a few justifications for having life insurance in the UAE.

Your dependent family members can maintain their standard of living without having to make sacrifices for their basic requirements according to a life insurance plan.

In the worst-case scenario, life insurance serves as your income.

A portion of many life insurance policies involves investments. You begin getting maturity benefits depending on your investment results after a predetermined duration.

Term life insurance protects your life against a huge guaranteed payment at a low insurance cost.

Permanent life insurance plans include a saving element and provide maturity rewards based on the cash value at the conclusion of the insurance period or as otherwise determined when the life insurance policy was purchased.

Your beneficiaries have a variety of payment alternatives, including the opportunity to apply the guaranteed sum to a current loan or mortgage. Alternatively, they might receive it on a regular basis based on their needs.

The insurance companies in the United Arab Emirates provide a quick and simple claim process to make things easier for your beneficiaries during trying times.

You may choose from a number of extra riders, such as critical and terminal disease coverage, accidental death benefits, and others, in addition to the basic protection.

Sam's personal advice and suggestion:

"Mr. & Mrs Kumar, since your latest new movie production is an action-packed adventure movie involving lots of stunts and action sequences in the open outdoors of Sharjah, hence I need you both to focus on taking "Whole life Insurance with accident riders". Meaning inclusion of untimely and premature death due to the accidents both while work and while living anywhere in the entire United Arab Emirates, the city of Sharjah being included too."

"The total amount to be insured is at your discretion and at the ability of your payments of premium in Dinars. Since you will be taking a Life Insurance Policy in the UAE, then your country of nationality laws that is India, cannot intervene or interfere in the outcome, claims and fulfilment of the policy.

This will be an international policy specially for important business people or high net worth individuals having either Indian passport or POI that is Person of Indian origin certificate or OCI that is Overseas Citizen of India. The life insurance policy is active and valid for claims only if the accident or death happens on UAE soil, while working or living in the United Arab Emirates."

Before taking our leave and permission to exit, Shamsuddin reminded us that, the Kumar's will have to be present in person to read, understand and sign all the necessary insurance policy document at the Sharjah head of office of the Insurance company.

"He reminded that he would be available in Sharjah during this coming weekend of Saturday and Sunday. Friday is their weekly off and Saturday is their first week day of business. If you both confirm your presence, then I can do all the necessary prepping and pre preparation, so that you will have a short and fast processing of your new insurance policy."

"Give us please a day or two" pleaded Bharat Kumar and we will get back to you soon with a confirmation. Sam's presented us his visiting card. First, he scribbled something on the back of the same business card. It read.

---

www.khairlegal.com

Sachaladevi was profoundly happy at the sudden turn of events. She had totally forgotten about the movie production house appraising her and the full movie staff, they it would be mandatory for one and all of the production staff to take either insurance of short term or long term or of the exact shooting duration schedule in Sharjah. This was made compulsory recently by the UAE Emirates government.

Sachaladevi went on to the terrace of her beach bungalow for some privacy and then dialled Suman Pandey's phone number. As always, he promptly took the call.

Sachaladevi explained to Suman in great detail the day's events and the visit of the Insurance solicitor Mr. Shamsuddin. She explained that she would be visiting Sharjah for this insurance policy formalities as she being a celebrity is not allowed group insurance as the other lower grade staff are doing. She is supposed to take individual life insurance, without it, which she would not be allowed to work legally on movie shooting sets in Sharjah.

"So, this phone call of yours, is for all of this excitement that you going to Sharjah alone over the coming weekend of Saturday and Sunday", Pandeyji enquired.

"A double yes". Sachala replied.

She further explained to Pandeyji, that he is due to provide some video presentation of what Bathroom solutions he intends to propose along with his quote, to her husband.

She continued explaining to Pandeyji, that she would have the perfect alibi of being in a foreign country on some business work. At that same time her husband Bharat Kumar would be perfectly all by himself, all alone at home at that secluded beach bungalow in Goa.

Slowly and very Spine Chillingly, it was dawning upon Pandeyji as to what Sachala was going say.

Then the cat jumps out of the bag:

"You have a genuine excuse to be present on your work assignment and appointment at my husband's house this weekend." "You will have Bharat Kumar a handicapped person, all by himself, all alone and you can plan and plot on some incident or accident that leads to the death of my husband."

Suman Pandeyji shouted angrily over the phone: *"What do you think, I am? I am an entrepreneur, not an exterminator or executioner."*

The phone line went suddenly dead at the other end. I was wondering, did see cut or did my call get dropped by the telephone exchange.

I would know for sure, by her calling back in a few minutes. But no call came back. So, I decided to phone her and recontinue the conversation to its logical conclusion.

I dialled back to her and then suddenly remembered her serious instructions. Never call. Always text or wait for my call. I immediately disconnected my call. At least she would receive a missed call notification I felt.

The entire day, there was absolutely no communication from Mrs. Sachaladevi. It was like I was a nobody or not existing person.

I did not like this. I remember Sachala saying, that she likes men that have control over their emotions. I decided to handle this practically and continue with Kumar's bathroom project professionally.

I still 4 more full days, to provide the final touches and finishing to Video presentation and to the Quotation and Job order contract. Everything was ready and on time.

For the first time, in this illicit relationship between Sachaladevi and myself, we both were fighting hard to take or be in control of the situation.

If Sachala did not care to chat or call. So, did I. But I was literally, whining and pining for her communication all day and night. During the day I could keep my mind busy with my shop or office staff and with customer complaints. But the night was the most difficult to cross over. From the sudden over consumption of alcohol, I slowly realized that I was becoming alcohol dependent during the nights.

Sachaladevi was out of sight, out of my body, but I could not remove her thoughts out of my mind. Why do we humans, not have the ability to delete the memories that are sour and bitter for us? All of the memories of the love-making with Sachaladevi which was wonderful, now seemed so painful to me both in body and mind. My balls were literally aching in desire to empty my seed into her vagina.

Monday – Silence from Sachala. Tuesday – Silence. Wednesday – Silence. Thursday – Silence

On Thursday morning, I decided to phone Bharat Kumar and fix an appointment for Saturday. That way I could physically see Sachala if she is there or gone to Sharjah.

"Sir Kumar. This is Pandeyji. Good morning. I need a time slot for tomorrow to meet you and update you upon your project video presentation and also need to provide you the quote cum contract for the Bathroom work order."

"How about 11 am tomorrow morning? Is that fine with you?" Kumar seemed to sound cheerful over the phone. He made no mention of Sachaladevi not being around. Was he happy like most husbands, to have their wives gone far away from them for a few days?

Surprisingly enough, after a few minutes of phone call conversation, I happened to receive a message from Sachaladevi.

After 4 full days of controlled silence, I was happy that it was she who was breaking down and not me. Excitedly I accessed my mobile phone, to know that it was not a text message but a Video message notification. I clicked on the play icon button and the video seemed to be large and was buffering and getting downloaded to my phone.

Finally, after a few minutes the video file got fully downloaded. It was a video recording of one of our love making rendezvous in my beach bungalow. The video recording quality was in 4k format and was brilliantly beautiful. This was the night, when Sachaladevi was in the mood for some role play. She wanted me to rough it out.

She desired to have rough sex. This was nothing new for me. Many women like to being fantasized being raped violently but in controlled circumstances. Sachala being a control freak, sort of so to say wanted our love making that day to be rough, real and like a rape. I happened to volunteer very eagerly.

Which man, would not in my place? It was interesting to know that she had recorded the entire rough sex love making of ours which truly looked like a forceful rape. I thought her sharing this video from Sharjah meant that she was missing my love-making. I was missing fucking her roughly too. Sachala's video share made my mood upswing and I felt nice. After an hour or so of receiving our sex video, received an international incoming call from Sachala. I was truly exhilarated. Excited to hear her dusky voice from Sharjah, I took her call. Without any pleasantries, she promptly came to the point.

"*Pandeyji, did you watch the video I shared to you?* Yes. I promptly replied.

She continued: *"How many times did you watch it?*

"A couple of times", I said. Sachaladevi: *"Good, very good."*

Next, she asked me: *"Did you enjoy viewing the Video?"*

"Yes. But it was more enjoyable doing it. Watching it was also good. Thanks for taking the recording for saving our memories and more thanks for sharing it to me, in your absence."

"Now listen very carefully," she said. *"Plan and plot an incident or accident that should lead to my husband's death this weekend when you are on official visit to my home. If you do not attempt at all, then this video will be shared to the Goa Police and the World Media. You violently and criminally raped me that night. It will be Celebrity Sachaladevi's word against yours. If the law does not kill you, one fanatic fan out of millions of my fans worldwide would suffice to violently kill you, I could cry and suggest that may Pandeyji be someday raped too."* I stood shocked out of my daylights and my phone fell from my hand. I picked it up and said hello. All that remained was a beep, beep beep, beeping terrifying sound.

♥

Chapter 3

Nothing lasts forever, not even love.

After Sachaladevi's phone call, I had to head home, leaving everything aside. Needed a cold chilling shower to cool me down and a large shot of whisky to stop my head from rolling.

Post showering, put on my daily night pyjamas and laid myself on the bed. I was staring at the circular moving blades of my ceiling fan. On each of the blades, I could see the jumbled alphabets, R, E, M D, U, R.

It was MURDER.

This is one thing that I had never done in my whole life. Killing a human in cold blood. Forget human. I never even ever killed any tiny animal for that matter. And here Sachaladevi was expecting me to kill her husband? What for? For her? Was she *really* so precious?

Sachaladevi had her prey that is me, perfectly trapped in a corner.

Problem was – Bharat Kumar – Alive.

Solution was – Bharat Kumar – Dead.

Scotland Yard Police, once had said: *"There has never ever been a perfect murder. Every murderer makes some fatal mistake."*

I did a SWOT analysis for my current situation. Something that I had learned in my college MBA days.

Strengths

His own wife was wanting his murder.
His wife was my lover.
His wife was the owner of all the assets. Post his death, her money would be my money too.
I have easy physical access to the house.
I have gained the professional and personal trust of Mr. Bharat Kumar.
I was strong and muscular. Kumar was fat and pot-bellied.

Weaknesses

I never had any experience in committing any murders.
I was not a professional killer.
I did not have easy access to arms and poisons.
I was in love with Sachaladevi

Opportunities

I could be marrying Sachaladevi
I could learn the ropes of the film industry and become a producer someday.
I could inherit Millions.
I could get loads of hot leads of customers from the Bollywood industry.

Threats

Hanged till death for plotting and executing a cold-blooded murder.
Possibility of life time jail.
Sachaladevi already blackmailing me
Sachaladevi betraying me
Sachaladevi killing me
Not getting even a rupee from Sachaladevi

There must be no error or even the tiniest of miscalculations, I had to warn myself. Unless I had a fool proof plan and a water tight alibi, that I could escape from murder only then I would kill him and get away with it, otherwise I mustn't try it.

The advantages from the SWOT analysis were far and few in-between. Money, lots of money matters the most.

With lots of disposable money, I knew It would make a giant different in my life.

Sweet success and Sachaladevi would be my mistress for life. Education I had, Training I learnt, Craftsmanship skills I got developed and the business acumen and knowledge, was part and parcel of my life. But, due to lack of financial resources or large loans and without any large working capital, I was in trouble. If I could only plot my way to accidentally manslaughter him safely, in a way that no one would suspect that I had done it.

Plotting the accidental death of Bharat Kumar was extremely difficult and bordering on impossibility. He was always in the safe confines of his huge home. He never went out of the house. He never even went to the top floor or terrace of the house.

Plus, there was always Martha the permanent in house cook and maid who was living in the premises.

Martha could be my best alibi. Her statement would be iron clad for the police.

Sachala was right. The opportune time was Saturday or Sunday. With herself in Sharjah, and Kumar alone, the probabilities of a mishap or accident happening could never be overruled.

How could I be present at the house and at the time of the murder event, at the same time have an iron clad strong alibi of not being inside the house?

There was no point in my killing him if I was to end up in the gas chamber. If I killed him, I meant to have Sachala her assets and lots if not all of her money.

I decided to visit Mr. Bharat Kumar on time, tomorrow morning and honour my business appointment.

Sir Bharat Kumar was sitting on the veranda, a glass of whisky in his hand. Seen him drinking alcohol for the very first time.

His face was red-faced and his eyes were red coloured. *'Sit down, Pandeyji,'* he said, waving to a chair near his. He took out a carton of cigarettes and offered me one packet. *'Have a smoke.'* I took one full cigarette packet and sat down. Here I was smoking with the man that I was preparing to murder. This gave a dirty and creepy feeling to me about myself. How much low could I go?

"Suman, I am in a difficult situation." This was the first time ever that Sir Kumar ever used or took my first name with respect. Otherwise always he called me Panda or Pandeyji.

"What would you do, if you found the darling of your dreams, the love of your life, the woman you married for life to be a big cheat. A two-faced snake all of her life. To find her betraying you all the days of your life."

Without much thinking, instinctively I replied: *"I would kill her, without any hesitation".*

"Sir Kumar, can I just clarify one important matter with you?" "Yes Please"

"I understand that your wife has betrayed you and become unfaithful to you after your accident and you becoming handicap, right?"

To my utter shock and surprise, he replies: *"No. She always was an unfaithful bitch"*

I could not believe my ears.

"Let me tell you, what is sadly wrong with my wife.", "The glitz, glory and glamour has hit head." She was madly in love always only for two, things. That is Money and Sex." "As you can see, that I am much older than her. As with growing age, I became weaker in bed and that gave her the excuse to meet her needs from any tom, dick and harry. Her need for money is infinity. Her desire for more sex is insatiable."

"Sir Kumar, but why are you disclosing all of this to me?

"Pandeyji, because she is not around, I can open up my wounds, woes and worries to you. She is one major control freak. She married me for my money only. When I made serious loses in the movie business, now she wants to use me to recover all of those losses"

"Use you, Sir Kumar, I just did not understand."

"Five years ago, Sachaladevi insisted and forcibly got me to take out an accident insurance policy of a few crores of rupees." "She got a certain man from an insurance company to meet and talk to me. He tried his sales best to coax me to take out a one hundred crore accidental coverage. To stop her from continuously irritating m, I took out the Accidental insurance policy."

He showed his teeth in a vicious, grimacing grin.

'Pandeyji, do you know what happened then? We went to a party. I got a little high and she insisted on driving. Like a fool I let her. I went to sleep. Somewhere up the mountain road she stopped, got out of the car to talk to a pal of hers who had stalled his car right across the road.

She set the parking brake or at least she said she did when the police questioned her. Anyway, the car rolled down the mountain side with me in it. It's taken me a long time to figure that one out. Do you know what I think now? I think she wanted the one hundred crore insurance pay off more than she wanted me".

"Pandeyji, I know that today you are going to show me the video presentation of the Bathroom that you have designed for my special handicap needs." "The bathroom project will get a little delayed, because I forgot or rather, I could not ask you for an extremely special or let's say a killer component feature to be added within the whole facility. I need the bathroom to be able to kill my wife."

"I am not like many of the women who fuck for free and then do not pay the plumber any of his professional fees for his workmanship and skills"

"So here are 50 lacs cash in black, this is only for adding a KILLER FEATURE *within the entire bathroom facility, which I could enable on my own, but would appear as accidental to any insurance or police probing agency."*

"Leave your bathroom work quote with me. Come and collect the 50% advance cheque of whatever you asked for, immediately tomorrow from me, before my wife comes back home." "The murder payment will be in Cash. The bathroom work payment will be in cheque."

Here I was in a very precarious situation. Standing on the precipice so to say. Whom should I believe? The woman I made love too or the handicapped man who backed up his story with hard cash. 5 million rupees in advance, just for an accidental killer feature in built in the bathroom. 5 million more on delivery.

Plus, no negotiations for any discounts on my asking price for the bathroom work. This just seemed too good to be true. Sachaladevi need not know anything about this.

The money in hand was worth more than promises of millions in her hairy bush

---

♥

Chapter 4

The "Killer" or "Kill her" Bathroom.

The very next day, on Sunday as suggested by Sir Bharat Kumar, I visited his beach bungalow sharp at 10 am. I presented the bathroom video presentation to Kumar and without any hesitation, he approved the project design and its cost too. As he had promised, he had kept fifty percent of quotation which worked out to 25 lacs or 2.5 million Indian rupees.

I had appraised Mr. Kumar that the entire Bathroom project would take 7 days of continuous work to complete it. He agreed to it. Every day a total of 15 workers were commuted to the site from Margao. Their working day started sharp at 8 am and ended by Sunset a little after 6 pm daily. Transportation was arranged daily and was on company expense.

After acquainting all the workers of their day's responsibilities, I was about to take my leave from Mr. Kumar. He gently reminded me, "It would be nice if you could complete the work max by Friday evening, as I am expecting Sachaladevi to be back from her Sharjah trip. So, I would like to surprise her with the new bathroom set up.

This worked perfectly fine for me too. She would have been too much of a distraction to me and an attraction to my team.

This was the first project, for which I applied a lot of minds to it. I attended entirely to the designing part. There were three more areas of attention. I separated them for my team. They were the developing the design team, the décor team and finally the delivering team. The delivering team was more of bathroom artisans, plumbers, builders, finishers etc.

My physical presence was really needed mainly at the developing time, where physical aspects were being developed from fresh. The décor could be changed and replaced, not the build-up or developed part. That would involve restructuring and starting all over from scratch.

The final testing stage, I had planned to bring in from some hospital a real "handicapped" person on a mechanized wheelchair to use the bathroom for real and give me feedback.

For what the costing had reached too, in that same amount, any sane person could easily by a 2 BHK apartment in any local residential colony of Goa.

Three words to describe the bathroom: Exquisite, Exclusive & Exotic.

The flooring:

The entire flooring was smashed and redone and refitted with the highest standard of non-slip tiles and also lots of embossed grain effect for any rubber tires to move swiftly over it.

The Ceilings:

The full 1000 square feet or 100 Square meters of bathroom area on the ceiling was fitted with the latest "Ceiling lift". Kumar could be lifted directly from his wheel chair in the bedroom and taken around in the ceiling lift, all around the bathroom while he attended to natures call.

Alternatively, this also was a "Wheelchair Drive In" bathroom. We had made a hole in the wall, connecting to the bedroom of Kumar with just a wooden door frame fitted, leaving the access fully open without a physical door.

The Washbasin

This wash basin was totally tailor made to the body size of Mr. Kumar. With the lift ceiling or while on wheel chair, the entire wash basin was a 360% wraparound basin fitted with round mirrors with the person in the center of it. Everything in this bathroom was either by touch, voice commands, sensors or by remote control. The only physical thing was the plastic remote. Not only the basin, but in the entire bathroom there was not a single tap, faucet or pipe visible to the naked eye. Those things were meant for the poor.

Full Size bar:

The bar was completely made from glass. No wood. No plastic. No concrete. This was done, so as to enable the person to see his exclusive alcohol without any barriers coming between him and his spirits.

This was a fully equipped bar, so it had everything albeit in Mini size. Mini kitchen, Mini Fridge, Mini freezer and much more.

The bar was set and placed in a wet area. It had glass stools for other handicapped guests, if the client was entertaining with him in the bathroom.

Surrounding the glass bar, was situated the Jacuzzi, Steam cubicle, Shower area and Bathtub.

The Wet area:

Every facility in the wet area was structure of obstruction free. Both the wheel chair and the ceiling lift could access any service easily.

Steam area:

For maximum impact the client had to be in the designated steam area. Since it was an open steam facility, the steam would get dispersed and distributed in the full wet area with minimum heat impact to those in the Jacuzzi, Shower and Bath tub. But they could enjoy the benefits of the steam, albeit from a safe distance.

The Shower area:

Unlike most other shower cubicles being built for handicapped customers, this shower was a totally unconventional one.

Unconventional for these reasons – It was a totally open shower area. No glass enclosure used at all. To stop the water spilling or splashing outside its designated area, real trees and dense plant foliage was used instead of glass. The shower features had everything that man or money could buy. Waterfall effect, Rains, full body pressure massage and even the base could store water like a mini tank, where the ceiling lift could, "dip" the client in and out of the water.

Recliners

Multiple recliners were placed at different places for general sitting and relaxation. All the recliners were fitted with special water proof and heat proof leathers. Only genuine animal skin leather could be used.

Jacuzzi

Generally, Jacuzzis are in square, round or rectangular in shape, but this one was done last with whatever empty space that was left to be used. So, the Jacuzzi ended up in a "Semi Circle" shape.

Commode:

Only the commode was tucked away in a corner, as it needed walls to keep any undesired smells away. To solve that issue a covered enclosure works best. For airfreshner sprays, exhaust fans, and a tiny high speed overhead fan to dissipate any smells. The entire bathroom was air conditioned, yet the above were necessary too. The main commode was specially imported from Japan. It was the latest and most modern tool made for any human's butts. It had a heater, a powerful built in bidget water sprayer, perfuming functions, a disposable butt wiper and hot air dryer. All one had to do is "poop" inside the commode and get up or be lifted up, if you are crippled. Not to forget the commode had its very own devoted remote too.

TV Screens:

There were 3 TV screens fitted in the bathroom. One large size in the Bar cum Wet area, second medium size tv in the dry section area and the smallest tv was straight facing the commode for the person sitting and shitting.

Folding Murphy Bed:

To utilize space at its best, a small single person murphy bed was enclosed within the wall. When closed, the backside of the bed had expensive art hangings. When closed it was a small sofa. When open it converted itself in a mini size comfortable bed.

Emergency Lingerie Wash:

Many clients, do not like their staff or maids to handle their dirty inner wears. So, on a thoughtful note, a large size IFB Automatic Washing machine, dryer and heater comprising of 2 units were placed within the bathroom. So, one could shower and wash their dirty linen, coming out in dried, hot & freshly washed lingerie too.

This was a killer bathroom, worth dying for.

Chapter 5

The love of money is the root of all evil.

By Friday, everything was complete and operational to a T. Thoroughly. The bathroom was ready for inspection and inauguration by Bharat Kumar privately as he pleases.

By late evening, all the formalities of handing over the bathroom too were completed. The final balance payment was also presented to me by Cheque much before Sachala arrived on the scene.

There was only one unexpected surprise.

Bharat Kumar, told me to meet him in the open-air parking lot in front of the house. He did this, when he wanted to speak something serious and this ensured privacy from listening ears and modern gadgets.

"Pandeyji, he remarked, do you remember that my wife had gone to Sharjah to take the legally mandatory work insurance for her future forthcoming film?" "Yes", I replied.

Kumar told me that a new development, totally outside his area of control had happened recently. I was wondering what. But he was going to tell me any moment.

"We cannot kill my wife in the newly built bathroom at home here in Goa, now"

"Why, but why" I asked, *"after all of this planning, plotting and preparations"*

Bharat Kumar's voice echoed in my head: *"Sachaladevi cannot die in India, she has to die in Sharjah."*

I was totally confused and confounded with this new development.

"Why the change of Venue, now" I asked.

"What Venue?" barked Bharat.

I forgot myself, that hanging around with Bollywood celebrities, my language and lingo too picked up words relating to their trade of events and happenings.

"I meant Venue of Death." Sir Kumar.

Bharat had a short and swift maniac full laughter. *"What a play of words"* he said.

I kept on wondering silently in my head. But why. Why change so suddenly and so soon and at the last moment, just before the implementation of our plan.

Kumar spoke as though he was anticipating my thoughts: *"My wife shared me a copy of her latest insurance policy taken in the UAE, just a few days back. She has taken the policy for a couple of hundred crores".* I did not dare to ask, for how many hundred crores. He was not stupid to tell.

"In Sachaladevi's new insurance contract, there's a very strict rider & disclaimer that, this insurance is purely for the duration of work-related stay period in the UAE. Hence any insurance claim if ever made for any of the hundreds of movie production staff team, the incident or accident or death has to have happened within the geographical borders of the 44 cities of the United Arab Emirates. The insurance contract stays binding and legal for the company only while the insured person is living or dead in UAE"

I was slowly, surely and silently digesting the contents of Sir Kumar's disclosure. I could smell the fireworks of celebration in my heart and mind. There was now, no need of me to murder anyone.

I continued listening to Bharat Kumar, whilst keeping a blank poker like face.

Then he requested, what I was eagerly waiting to hear finally: *"I need you to immediately and urgently disconnect and discard the killer feature in your delivered bathroom"*.

I took that excuse and left him alone. Saying that I better get it immediately done before Sachala arrives on Sunday. I told him that, I need only a couple of hours to deactivate, dismantle and discard it permanently. I told him a lie. And a half-truth at the same time. I told him not to use the shower facility for just 2 days only. It would be okay to use the shower facility from Monday onwards. This information misguided him and he mistakenly self-understood that the killing feature was included within the shower facility.

My heart and mind were celebrating. Time and tide were working in my Favor. Also, Sir Kumar did not demand for the 50 % advance paid to be returned. That was really nice of him.

But slowly the fireworks in my mind ended. As it dawned upon me, with the arrival of Sachaladevi on Sunday, she would demand from me, some plot or plan or progress of a killer feature enshrined within the bathroom to kill her husband. Nothing changed the situation that she coldly blackmailed me into killing her husband. 50 % of the situation was still the same.

My mind was repeatedly telling me. Stall for time. Stall for time. Stall for time.

Time heals everything it is said. I just needed time to change my circumstances. How I truly wished, that I had not followed this lead of my dear friend Achut Pednekar.

My decision of following this lead was for more money. Sachala wanted to kill her husband for the freedom to spend her own money. Bharat Kumar desired freedom too from his control freak wife, but then changed his mind for more money.

We all felt, that we took or made decisions, but it was the motivating greed of more money that lured our decisions.

Sunday came and went. And first thing on Monday morning at 10 am, we were both seated in front of each other at our usual place, "Organic Coffee Café" at Anand Ashram.

Anand Ashram was no more a bundle of joy to both of us. Rather it reminded us of the foreboding thorns and thistles in all of our relationships. We decided, that next time we would meet at some touristy beach shack on Pollem beach or any other lesser crowded beach.

Sachaladevi, was no longer my diva, deva or devi for me. She did not appear anymore sexy or seductive to me. She having blackmailed me and threatened to throw me under the bus killed all my desires for her. I thought that I loved her. But truly lust lasts much longer than love.

As soon as the waiter left us to consume our hot coffee's, she without wasting any time, came back to business, demanding me as to what I had done during her absence. Referring to the bathroom development.

"Did you see and have a good look at the finished bathroom?" I enquired of her.

"Yes. Its luxurious, no doubt. But I wanted you to build a bathroom to KILL AND NOT TO THRILL."

Her choice of words, amazed me: *"Build a Bathroom to kill and not to thrill"*

"Yes, it's done", "But"

Sachaladevi asked: *"Why the but, what's the but for?*

"We will have to wait patiently for at least 6 months to pass. Why 6 months you will surely ask? This is because all of the Electric gadgets fitted have a 1-year warranty and all of the electronic gadgets fitted have a 6 months warranty towards failure."

"Also, if an accident immediately happens leading to someone's death, too soon after the building and installation of the new bathroom facilities, then the police investigation will easily suspect me and my activities. I will totally come under their scanner. Turn your head slowly & smartly and see all the overhead cameras fixed here at Organic Coffee Café."

For the very first time, I saw the tinge of fear on Sachaladevi's face.

I told her, that we both are not professional killers. We are victims of our own circumstances. If your husband's death who is a celebrity by himself, happens, the CID police won't waste much time in easily finding us meeting regularly here. They will have hard core video evidence.

Slowly the "joy stick", of control so to say, moved back again to my side. In my control. Sachaladevi definitely appeared scared. I was sure what was happening in her mind.

She was thinking. If the cops, get our personal meeting videos, outside so often, then the blackmailing rape video would appear to them to be more like a rough sex video.

"So, what's the solution, to this situation, Suman? Her husky, dusky and sexy voice slowly making a comeback. I did not show any reaction. Few minutes back, Sachaladevi was the demanding diva. Now she was trying to become to me, my Sachala again.

"I have friends in the security camera business and during a general conversation, here is what I found about security camera installations here in Goa".

Sachala was now paying total attention to what I had to say.

Her body was not in my control anymore. What was more important to me was now controlling her mind.

I thought to myself silently: *"Fucked her body, now Screw her mind."*

I continued telling her what I carefully wanted to tell. By general industry standards, all products and gadgets come with some default standards. Something similar to when we buy our new Android Smart phones. It is also called as "Factory Settings" in the case of phones.

Now coming back to security cameras, all commercial establishments are mandatory and compulsorily required by law to legally have a DVR connected to the establishment cameras. The purpose of all cameras is to collect video recordings as evidence. Video recordings need a huge amount of storage space. More space if the video is of 4K HD standard and if it is in full color recording. Hence the DVR (Digital Video Recorder). This is where the videos are stored for future record and reference.

Now comes the very important part:

All the time, I was doing the talking, and Sachala was quietly listening and absorbing everything. It was like for the first time I had mesmerised her or hypnotized her with my attention to detail. She suddenly stiffens her pose and becomes more alert.

I purposely take a pause. She could not bear the suspense.

"What is the important part" she asked.

I had her attention. I had her ears all open to my information. This was the right time to create, "inception" in her mind. She has to believe some factual information that I need to impress on her mind.

"Every Digital Video Recorder is made of a hardware called as a hard drive. This is where the videos are stored. Now pay attention."

I said the above words, now pay attention more to both her conscious and sub conscious mind.

"No commercial especially the smaller establishments can afford to store all the video data of all the years on a hard drive. Not physically sensible and not financially viable."

"Under the Information Technology Act (updated) of 2000, It is mandatory and legal for all shops, offices and establishments coming under commercial business licences to store the videos for a minimum of 1 full month or 30 days."

"But remember, by default most of the DVR's that come out of the manufacturing units in India are keeping themselves more compliant and safer in the ambit of law, by enabling the DVR to record and save videos for a longer period of 3 months."

Sachala was keenly keeping pace with what I was saying and sharing. It seemed to be making sense to her and hence she popped the query:

"What happens after the passage of 3 months?"

I needed to push the right buttons of Sachala, hence I praised her saying: *"Interesting and Intelligent Question"*.

I told her that after 3 months, the hard drive loops back to the starting position on the hard drive's disk and starts recording the new and relevant videos all over again.

"What happens to the old videos?" Sachala asked.

"They get over written or in other words, the older videos get automatically deleted and then the very current and present new videos are stored in that same sectors of the disk."

"So, after a full period of 90 days of recording, our meeting videos will automatically get overwritten, deleted and discarded without any human control." Sachala asked.

"Yes". I had to say so.

Slowly her demure personality was leaning again towards the demanding Sachala. I had to take control. I had to do something.

"Oh. I forgot one very important thing".

"What is it?", she asked.

Most modern-day establishments tend to have a backup of a hard drive back up. This is an optional feature and not compulsory by law.

"This can be declared or declined upon, during the time of investigation."

"Since many hardware DVR tend to malfunction or break down, hence some establishments having educated owners, tend to take some free or paid "Cloud Storage Service" over the internet. Since there is unlimited space on the internet. The is no need of any feature or facility to over write the saved videos. This is a total personal and private facility that is ONLY accessible to the owner or more accurately to whoever owns the Email Id and the connecting password for the cloud service".

So, if the owner of this "Organic Coffee Café" has registered and connected his security cameras to some internet cloud service, then our multiple meetings will be immortalized forever on some file and folder over the internet servers.

At the back of both of minds, two different thoughts were occurring at the same time: Sachala wondering how to retrieve the internet recordings and delete them forever. Suman thinking how to retrieve the internet recordings and save them as a safety net.

Sachala's demeanour was back to her sexy and seductress woman that she was before she left for Sharjah. I too heaved a sigh of relief.

"It does make total sense to what you have said. That means, we will have to wait a little more than 6 months to activate our killing machine."

"Yes. Exactly". This is the stalling time, that I badly needed.

Then out of the blue, Sachaladevi seriously apologised to me.

"Suman, you do not know, under how much duress I have gone through in this failed marriage of mine with Bharat and now the excruciating stress of this killing business of killing my husband, the man I once loved."

"With folded hands, I want to say Sorry to for blackmailing you and threatening you. At that time, I have to sincerely admit that I meant it. But now I am deeply regretting. Please do accept my apologies and forgive me if you can?"

For the first time in my life, I found the most beautiful, the sexiest actress and one of the wealthiest women from Bollywood, admitting her mistakes and saying sorry to me.

Like cold ice cream in her warm hands, my heart melted. At that very moment, she held my both arms on the restaurant's table. I tried pulling it away, saying. *"Be careful, it will get recorded."*

Without any hesitation and without any signs of fear, she remarked: *"I care a fuck. And you said nah. 90 days and it will disappear". "I love you".*

I Love You

Hearing those three magical words, was like being striked by a lightning bolt. Again, so soon, it was the same situation. Fight. Flee or Freeze.

I just could not believe my luck. I was nothing. Just a small business entrepreneur in Goa. Only the commercial people of South Goa knew me. And here the heart throb of Millions of fans world-wide and the wife of Bollywood producer Mr. Bharat Kumar declared her love for me.

As I was basking and soaking in the sunshine of my new found love.

She asked me back, *"Don't you have to something to say in return?"*

I bluntly told her: *"If you are accepting me to say in return, I Love You Too." "Then sorry, no."*

"Because, I Love You Too MUCH".

Glancing around and finding an empty early morning restaurant, Sachaladevi pulled her chair closer to me and without any signs, she pulled my head in both of her hands, closer to her face and kissed me gently, but quickly on my lips.

Before I could warn her of anything, she said. *"Fuck the cameras".*

We surely had kissed earlier many times, more passionately but more privately. But this one she did in public, especially for the cameras, instilling in me genuine confidence that she truly loves me.

She was risking everything for me. Her life. Her career. Her Husband. Literally everything.

This seemed to be the best day of my life. But it was just the beginning.

Then she declared that she had bought a special gift for me all the way from Sharjah. I was wondering what the heck would it be.

She held my hand and then she tugged me to follow her. We walked out the café towards her parked car and from a distance she opened, the boot of the back of her car.

It was dark, and I could not see much. She groped inside and pulled an expensive looking stainless-steel briefcase, something similar used by photographers to protect their expensive cameras and lenses.

She asked me to carry it back to our table. On reclining back in our seats, there was an extreme confused and curious look on my face, while Sachaladevi's face was beaming with excitement.

I was just silent and staring at my gift that she brought from Sharjah.

"Open it up", "It's yours now." "Please do go ahead."

As though I was unwrapping a cuddled infant in arms, I slowly opened the briefcase. To my utter joy and surprise, there was a full-size whisky bottle.

LE CLOS WHISKY - The Macallan 1926

"Sachala, If I am not mistaken. This happens to be one of the rarest and most expensive whiskies in the whole wide world. Oh my God!"

I just could not believe my eyes. I had to pinch myself to wake myself from this dream. I did so and Sachala had a good laugh seeing me pinching myself on my arm.

"Permit me Sachala, to check the price of this whisky on Google."

"Check it up, if you wish too. It's so special. That you are one of the only two men in the whole wide world who will be having it and drinking it too."

I did a quick Google search and here is what I found:

The luxury spirits retailer Le Clos has set a world record after selling two extremely rare bottles of the famous whisky, The Macallan 1926, for $1.2m in its store at Sharjah International airport.

I read the above out loud. *"That one customer was me Sachala said. I requested total anonymity while buying the bottle, hence my name has not come on that latest internet news report."*

She saw me opening the Calculator widget on my I Phone. *"Calculator will not be able to calculate the price for you. It will give an error."*

"Whatever the price may be, Suman, its priceless for me. Just like you."

The business man inside of me, could not stop me from googling for the exchange rate of 1.2 million Dollars in Indian Rupees.

1,200,000 USD = 100,832,340 INR

"What the fuck is gone wrong with you Sachala? This bottle of whisky costs in Indian rupees 10 Crores and 83 lacs. Are you gone mad?"

"So true Suman. So true." *"I am madly in love with you".*

"Don't let the businessman inside you start thinking: One thing Suman, this bottle is yours now. But not to sell it off, but to drink it with me and celebrate our love."

Suddenly, out of nowhere, Sachala demanded for her gift in return. The day was not ending with its surprises.

"Don't tell me you forgot. Remember the first time we made love, in the tank. I asked you for a gift, that all the money in this world cannot buy. Your original poetry on our first love making."

"Oh, yes," I lied. *"I have scribbled something but not to total satisfaction"*

Sachala got up to leave. She gave me a tight hug, while whispering in my ears, *"When the poetry is ready, call me"*.

After Sachala left. I called to the waiter and asked for the bill. Instead of the waiter, the restaurant manager came and very graciously and courteously mentioned that the bill has been paid and cleared in advance.

"Madam also paid for all the other table covers. She had reserved the entire restaurant just for the two of you Sir".

That input, told me a lot. No wonder the entire restaurant was empty today, during peak morning breakfast time. Hence Sachala confidently kissed me in the restaurant openly. I thought to myself.

While driving back another thought entered my mind. Could Sachala have purchased the entire management and making sure that the cameras too were put off, whenever we met at their restaurant". Anything was possible with Sachaladevi.

Sachaladevi did not scare me. *Her attention to detail frightened me.*

♥

Chapter 6

Maid in Heaven

During the seven days of bathroom work undergoing on at the Kumar's residence, I had total access to come and go anytime during the day to inspect the quality of my team workers.

This was the first and only time, that I happened to have to talk to the family's permanent cook and maid. She was the cook responsible for all the families' eating habits, right from breakfast until dinner and desert.

The two daughters of the Kumar's family were always studying at some international hostel, so that they could be kept far away from the fights and squabbles of this broken couple.

I never ever gave sufficient due thought, to interacting with the female help of the house, wondering of what use it could be to me. Now I was slowly realizing, that it is always the house servants who are ears and eyes to all the skeletons in every family cabinet.

All this time, I was never introduced to the maid of the house. There genuinely was no need for that.

But now, Martha had voluntarily taken over the responsibility and duty of providing breakfast, lunch and evening tea to all of my 15 staff daily for one full week. The Kumar's had absolutely no objection to this. This would get the workers back to their assignments on time after their lunch or snack break.

She was not doing all of this work alone, I later understood.

She had her very own team of workers, but they were restricted to an outhouse which was actually a Portuguese looking Goan house at a stone's throw away.

The other night, that I was with Mrs. Sachaladevi on the terrace and tank, I happened to see and notice the lights on in a Mangalorean tiled roof house. I thought to myself, that it must be some immediate neighbouring family in the village.

But it was not so. That Goan house was the permanent residence for all of the other support staff, cleaning staff, cooks and administrative office staff too. The ground floor Martha told me was entirely set up as an office, just like in the corporate company style. In the front section is the office, at the back are the storage rooms. On the first floor are individual separate rooms for all of the staff. The floor is unisex, without any further gender-based divisions of male or female.

The Kumar family it seems, were very liberal and lenient and they allow their staff to bring in friends and family on visits, but matters should be discreet and privately managed.

Martha, it seems was the only oldest staff of the Kumar family. She had been the nanny – a professional care taker to both the daughters of Sachaladevi. It was impossible for Sachala to be a full-time mother and full-time actress. So, she had to sacrifice at lot at home to achieve a lot in the outside world.

Martha never ever spoke any unkind word against the Kumar family. In return the Kumar family, during official hours and especially in front of strangers or outsiders like me, she was decently treated like a staff, but in their private time, she was treated lovingly just like family.

Besides cooking and cleaning, if Martha loved to do anything was talking.

This was because during the working hours, she had to act professional and keep the mouth zipped in front of important visitors. I decided to let her continue talking to her hearts content, sooner or later she would spill out some teeny meeny bit of information that could mean millions to me.

Just two days had passed, and all of my 15 staff were speaking very highly of Martha's cooking skills. So much that, one of my contractors was enticing her to work as a partner in a restaurant that his brother was planning to open in North Goa. She totally shut him up, when she told him that the Kumar family built a duplex bungalow for her on her ancestral land in Goa, gave her an expensive new car and took care of her children's foreign educational fees. If that is not enough, she said, *"If I tell you my monthly salary, you will feel embarrassed at how much less, you may be working for Pandeyji".*

Martha, not only knew to feed mouths, she also had the teeth to bite and keep the idiots mouth shut.

She also ended up telling me, that she was the only staff that had two quarters to stay. Before Sir Kumar's accident, she used to stay only during the day here at the main beach bungalow and used to retire for the night at her first-floor room at Goan staff out house.

I am recounting and retelling whatever I could scrape out from my communication with Martha throughout the week.

On the third day, I informed Martha, that I will be there for lunch in the afternoon, to which she immediately without any fear, refused. *"No Sir. Are you gone mad?" Sachaladevi will kill me, if she knows that I served you along with the other staff of yours? Nah re baba. No"*

I pleaded to her, that all the staff were praising her food and saying that it was too delicious, finger licking delicious.

"No staff food, for you Sir." "You are a special person for Madam and Sir."

This woman was making me wonder. Did she know or suspect of my affair with her Madam Sachaladevi? I just could not tell.

Then she sprang a tiny surprise.

"If you want to taste my food, then I would like to cook something special for you Sir. If it's okay with you, then you can come on Saturday as Madam is back from Sharjah so I can take an early off on Saturday to my other room in the outhouse. It's a very tiny room on the terrace, exclusively for me. I call it my very own penthouse. From my window, I can view the entire Kumar bungalow crystal clearly at any time."

What is this woman trying to tell me? Did she genuinely have a vantage view point from her room overlooking the Kumar's bungalow. Did she ever happen to see me coming and going on those nights of my fucking sprees with Suchala?

All of my above questions would get answered and cleared by paying her a casual visit late on Saturday night.

I hope, this would not anger the Kumar's family, to know of me hanging around and interacting with the staff of their house. Any way's I had received the payment for my bathroom services in full. So, there was nothing to worry about.

Anything that I could find on the internet or in movie magazines was very glossy and flavourful. I was digging for dirt. Not for diamonds. Not for anything soulful, but definitely something sinful to nail the coffin to the ground, so to say.

My main purpose, for hanging around Mrs. Martha was to somehow make a key copy of the main beach bungalow door.

That was my cake. Any other information from Martha would be like a "Cherry on the Cake".

Saturday morning came and I was totally at a loss of what to wear for dinner to Martha's room? Shall I take my car or my bike? What appropriate gift to give her for her kind dinner gesture? Would it be considered indecent going to the Maid's house so late at night? What about Sir Kumar, he would be left all alone the whole night at the beach bungalow?

Should I tell Sachaladevi of my dinner treat from her Maid Martha? What if Martha has already told Sachaladevi and taken permission from her?

By early afternoon, I self-answered all of my questions to my own self-satisfaction.

I decided to wear some casual picnic design short sleeve shirt. And half size denim jeans shorts.

Going on a bike, would be better, not to make the maid feel small.

Martha herself invited me late at night after her chores got over at the Kumar's residence. Plus, she needed some extra time to cook for our dinner meal. Also, she would be fully aware, of the sensibilities of Sachaladevi and Bharat before calling me to her room.

Sir Kumar, would not be all alone as Mrs. Sachaladevi was back from Sharjah.

I will carefully ask Mrs. Martha if Sachaladevi knows about our dinner meeting tonight.

My agenda for meeting Martha was short and simple.

Firstly, I needed digitally scanned copies of her main set of keys for the beach bungalow. I was carrying on my body a small pocket scanner.

Secondly, I wanted to see the view from Marthas room window. This could be a dangerous future scenario, if she knew of my nightly visits to Kumar's residence.

Thirdly, she loved to talk, so was hoping to someway delight her in voluntarily giving out some personal or private information on the Kumar's. Bollywood knew how to hide its dirt.

I had to search for diamonds. The dirt would automatically come out first.

I suddenly realized, that we had not shared each other's mobile phone numbers, so there was no way to get in touch or to contact her for last minute instructions.

Saturday evening came. I had lots of time on hand. So, I decided that I was dressed casually and it made me feel touristy. The sun was just about to set at the Cavellossim beach. The blue skies were turning greyish and then dark. Around, 7 pm, having crossed a little ahead of the Donna Slyvia Resort, noticed and loud and colour board shouting in more vivid color, the name "Mike's Place". I decided to take a left turn and I turned by Royal Enfield Interceptor towards the left internal village lane proceeding towards, Mike's Place.

Mike's Place was actually a huge modern Goan residence bungalow that had been converted into a full-fledged Goan Sports Bar. The design at the entrance itself was very flashy and colourful. Every inch and pinch of the boundary walls, the house walls, the coconut trees, the table covers, everything was shouting and screaming and had something nice to say.

The owner positively believed in using every bit of space for advertising. It was one big bright spot, that could not be missed even on a dark stary night. It seemed as though all the celebrities and stars were to be seen at Mike's place this weekend. I choose the corner most and quietest table far from the buzz of the peppy and chirpy youthful crowd.

I decided to guzzle a couple of Kingfisher Premium Beers along with a couple of plates of French fries to keep me busy whiling away my time.

After 4 beers down, I saw the time on my wristwatch showing 09 pm. I decided I better leave Mike's Place, before all the local shops close their shutters for the day.

I requested the waiter for the bill, cleared it, left a generous tip and promised him to leave a positive review for the excellent live music band performing that evening.

Now I had the difficult task of finding to buy and take something sensible for the Maid Martha. My mother always used to tell me. *"Never ever go empty to any guests house, especially if you are visiting them for the very first time."*

I happened to find, D'Mello's K4 Supermarket at Luisa by the Sea, Shopping center complex, Mobor beach. Mobor is the next and last beach before the landmass gets separated by the Betul river and Estuary. It turned out to be a "One Stop Shop" with all things available under one roof. This place turned out to be a last-minute shopping blessing to me.

So, what did I shop for the Maid Martha? A mixed assortment of chocolates, a Banyan Tree Wine bottle from Mahabaleshwar vineyards and an Amul brand Ice Cream Cake. Good that I carried by empty laptop backpack to accommodate carrying all of these gifts.

I ensured to keep the pocket scanner, in a separate pouch of the laptop bag, not to accidently remove it in front of Martha.

To reach to the Kumar's guest house, I used the Google Maps facility and found that I would have to take an immediate first internal road lane before the one that I take to reach the Kumar's beach bungalow.

I reached the intended left lane, a little after 9.45 pm and was surprised to see sufficient road lamps on with their white led lights shining bright on the dark Goan roads.

The entire internal lane was totally filled with dust and sand from the Cavellossim beach winds.

My breath definitely had the smell of wheat oats beer.

There was a nice cool winter breeze in the October air.

From far away, I could see a yellow bulb incandescent light from the terrace room of the guest house. It appeared as the rest of the staff were apparently tired from their daily duties and had retired to their rooms for the night. People in Goa do really go to sleep, pretty early I should say.

The Kumar's guest house was standing tall on a slightly elevated hill, whereas the Kumar's Beach Bungalow was built on the sandy sand dunes.

As I approached the property, I could see the faint silhouette of a female figure standing outside patiently for me. It had to be Martha.

I was a wee bit nervous. Dunno for what. I prayed that the food of the maid was good if not heavenly divine.

Martha was standing with a lit torch to light my way. My Bullet Bikes headlight flooded on her full body. I could see a very different Martha. Martha the Maid, but without her daily official uniform on her body. She was wearing some well-cut dress, that made her look slimmer and taller.

Now I understood why I was feeling nervous.

The way I felt and expressed myself matched similarly to the lyrics of the world-famous song, "Hotel California".

On a dark desert highway, cool wind in my hair

Warm smell of colitas rising up through the air

Up ahead in the distance, I saw a shimmering light

My head grew heavy and my sight grew dim, I had to stop for the night

There she stood in the doorway, I heard the mission bell

And I was thinkin' to myself, "This could be heaven or this could be hell"

Then she lit up a candle and she showed me the way

There were voices down the corridor, I thought I heard them say

I warned myself, that I should not be too overly late in leaving and without fail not to have an overnight stay.

As I got down from my Bullet Enfield Interceptor bike, I was greeted with the most warm and glowing smile that any woman could give. I reciprocated in the same way. She welcomed me to follow her and was expressing gratefulness for coming and more importantly for coming on time.

As we were walking, I noticed a small dilapated chapel along the way. It was very nondescript and it looked like it was not spiritually active in any way. As though she read my mind, Martha commented on the chapel that we were walking by. Saying that it was an ancient monument from the Portuguese era.

After walking for a little while and I noticed that it was all the time an incline. Then we came across a huge boundary wall that ran parallel for a mile or more. Martha commented again, as long as this boundary wall goes, all of the land is the property of Mr and Mrs Kumar. The main purpose of the wall is to segregate Work from Home. The company staff keeps on changing on a hire and fire basis, so they are not welcome or encouraged to walk over to the private area of the Kumar's bungalow. I behave like a mediator between the staff and the family. This is the way how celebrities live in Goa.

The torch carried by Martha surely helped us. I had to ask out of curiosity as to where were all of the staff. Pat came her reply, *"It's the weekend nah. So, most of them love to head to their homes in and around South Goa. Since all the company staff work only 05 days every week, it does tend to get very quiet on the weekends. Someday come on any weekday and you will see the opposite of this. It becomes like a Goan fish market, many a times".* She gave out a tiny laughter that broke the silence all around us.

At the main, teakwood door, she put her right hand into her deep dress pocket and out came one big bunch of keys. OMG. I said in my mind. How to recognize the keys to Mr. Kumar's beach bungalow from this fat bunch. This is gonna be a difficult task.

To get some reaction from her, I said: *"That's one big bunch of keys that you are carrying in your pocket."* She replied back naturally: *"Oh, that's only the bunch of keys of this guest house. The bungalow keys are in another much smaller bunch."*

To hear that was a lot of relief.

As we pushed the door inwards, I realized that we were the only 2 souls in this huge Portuguese looking Goan house. To confirm the same. I said, *"You could have rung the doorbell, for someone to open for you." "That's not possible as there is no one in the full building."* Replied back Martha.

Martha said, *"We do not have the facility of an elevator here. So, you will have to give some exercise for your legs. Shall we take the stairs?"*

"Yes, after you Mrs. Martha." I replied.

She retorted back. *"Sir Suman. Please do call me Martha only. As my husband is long dead around 5 years back. I am a widow now."*

"I will call you by your first maiden name of Martha, only if you drop that unnecessary title of Sir"

"And," I am so sorry to hear about your husbands' demise." I spoke.

"No need to be. Sometimes death can be a blessing and many a times an incident or accident can bring new blessings in your life."

"Martha. If it's not too personal and private, how did your husband die?

"Oh, I thought that since you are close to Mrs. Sachaladevi that she must have told you by now,

Again, there it comes once more. The faint hint of a taunt. So faint, so well delivered casually that it did not qualify to be called a sarcasm too.

Then the bombshell of a news hits me hard:

"My alcoholic husband was working as a permanent driver for Sir Bhart Kumar." "Outside duty times too they both were drinking buddies. They both were friends with the bottle."

We are talking as we were climbing the steps to her terrace private penthouse room. I noticed that each storey had very good height between each floor, being built from the Portuguese times. Higher the height, designated as richer the person.

Martha continued: *"On that fateful party night, as they were always drunk, I just don't know how things turned pretty ugly, pretty fast. Sachaladevi had got down from the car to help some friend whose car had broken down while driving down the hill. My drunk husband and Sir Kumar who was more drunk too, somehow went rolling down the hill that fateful night. My husband died. Bharat sir survived the accident but was left marred for life."*

I have to mention, something that I totally forgot: All of my conversations with Martha were not in the English language. She loved speaking in local Indian language of Hindi, I thought maybe because she liked Hindi movies and also, because she was working with Bollywood stars, one who was a pure North Indian.

Language does break down a lot of barriers. Martha a Catholic Christian from Goa, myself an Aryan Hindu from Uttar Pradesh, felt very comfortable in the presence of Martha who was speaking Hindi very fluently and elegantly. Something not so happening with most Goans in Goa.

Her single self-attached room on the terrace was more like a decent studio apartment, but I let her call it her pent-house.

As we entered in her private staff room, I suddenly felt my hands empty and realized that I had left Martha's gifts on my Bullet bike petrol tank.

I rushed back down, collected the gifts hanging in the laptop bag that I usually keep when its heavy on the petrol tank.

While walking back, uphill, there I could see Martha in the only yellow backlit bulb light of her room. I realized then, if the lights in her room were off, then she could see everything outside clearly, but no one could notice her standing at the window, looking outside.

With that disturbing thought in the back of my mind, I profusely apologised to her. She told me that he had not to worry, as the bag would remain there as it is, while returning back home.

That's the time I told her. *"These are some gifts that I picked up from some local store. I hope you like them. Excuse me Martha, as I am not good at buying gifts for females."*

She responded: *"Which female in the world hates a beautiful bouquet of flowers.? Then she saw the chocolates."* She had a small snack of Goan Cashewnuts from her very own plantation brought as a snack for me. So, she offered me, saying, *"Sweet for the sweet and Nuts for the nut." I will eat your Sweets, you eat my Cashewnuts."*

I did not want to add any comment to that.

She continued opening her gift hamper. Then her hands picked up the Banyan Tree Wine Bottle. This she quietly kept on her side table stand.

Finally, she picked up the last item from my laptop bag. The Amul Ice Cream Cake. As soon as she had opened the cake in her hand, her eyes became moist and tears started rolling down her fair cheeks.

Now I was left wondering, what the heck in the world could make any female to cry on seeing a cake.

Then I thought out loudly. *"By any chance, Martha is today your birthday anniversary?"*

"No. Not at all." No way. It's not my birthday."

"Today is the birthday anniversary of my daughter. Just a little while before you arrived, I spoke to Jennifer. She is studying and attempting her MBBS and MD medical degree from Croatia near Russia."

A small idea came to my mind. I took my ball point pen, without pressing the point outside, then with the tip of the pen, I scratched on the cake in tiny cursive handwriting and wrote.

"Happy Birth Day to Jennifer in Croatia"

"With lots of love, kisses and hugs. Your Mum Martha."

I found from my phone's music gallery a happy birthday song. Took my cigarette lighter kept the blue flame in continuous on mode. Then stuck the tiny plastic lighter into the cake as though it was candle. I played the happy birthday song in the background while Martha and I sang along. I took the video of this cake and shared it to her.

I requested Martha to send this song to her daughter immediately. It was my small birthday gift for her.

Martha's joys knew no bounds. She felt very happy with the turn of events. I reminded her that she needs to keep the Ice Cream cake in her refrigerator, otherwise it will melt all over.

It made sense to her. She dutifully got up and attended to the cake, saying we will eat it as a desert after our dinner.

I found this time, as a good opportunity to have a look outside from one her windows. The guest house property was situated on an elevated hill. Plus, the room of Martha was on the second floor of this house. I walked myself to the closest window and had a look outside.

What I saw shocked the daylights out of me. From where I was standing, I could see, without any obstruction of any trees or man-made structure a direct crystal-clear view of the Kumar's beach bungalow from a higher perspective. Even in this pitch, darkness, I could see very clearly without straining my eyes at the tank, the terrace and the whole right – angle structure. Any person, entering or going out from the bungalow could be shot even by an amateur like a shooting duck. Plus, today was not a full moon night, like the night I and Sachaladevi made love on the terrace and the tank.

If Martha happened to be in her pent house room, that night, then there happened to be a great chance of her seeing me and Sachaladevi on the terrace. Goodness gracious.

I felt a very sickening feeling in my stomach as my heart was coming up in my throat. As calm and composed Martha seems to appear, she was surely being very mysterious and creepy.

I got the feeling, I was invited to this dinner, not really for the food, but to see the window view and to understand the seriousness of the situation.

Martha was surely trying to communicate something to me. But her ways were very unsettling and unnerving to me. It's like in a game of cards, she knows she has a very strong hand, but does not know how to play her cards safely and smartly.

From the kitchen, I could hear the sounds of utensils being heated and food was being prepared for dinner.

Martha came to ask me: *"Suman, do you want dinner to be served or would you like me to open your wine bottle for us to drink? Do you have to reach home early, maybe your wife will be waiting for you at home?"*

Martha was surely checking about me upfront: I liked it that way, rather than hitting around the bush.

"Martha, just like you I am living alone by myself, as I am a bachelor for life. So, I don't have anyone waiting for me at home" "I will leave whenever you tell me to get lost. I said with a small chuckle, I am very good at getting lost."

"Good to know that you are not bounded by any woman waiting at home or bounded by the boundaries of time". "You seem to be a smart man who treasures his freedom the most"

Martha came with a large tray full of savouries which looked mostly home prepared and two empty wine glasses.

Just like a good cook, she started explaining to me the dishes kept in front of me. That's bread fruit an exotic local vegetable exported in large numbers to all European countries. The bread fruit is half cooked then air fried. The next dish is Batter fried Brinjal. Dipped in wet gram flour, then patted with dried bread crumbs and deep fried in North Indian Sesame Oil. The third are Potato wedges with lots of Jeera and Garlic flakes on it. The wedges are baked. Finally, the fourth snack is Gobi Manchurian but with genuine Cauliflower and not Cabbage as it is done in street food stalls all over Goa.

"Martha. You did not have to take so much trouble in making such a delectable spread." And that too this is just the Snacks & Savouries. Please tell me if I am mistaken.

"Suman. You are absolutely right. You are not mistaken."

"You are never mistaken. Because you never have got married. Only married men are mistaken".

"Martha. Come again. I did not get you. Sorry. I mean, I did not understand you."

"Suman. It's so simple. To be married you have to TAKE a MISS in Marriage. But you have not done that. So, you have not committed the sweet MISS TAKE of Marriage."

I had a hearty laugh at the comical play of words. I laughed till my eyes welled up in tears.

"Please do open the bottle and pour us both the wine. Make me a small one as I tend to get drunk fast." Said Martha.

"Equal pegs for equal people. You are single. I am single. You are Sweet and Beautiful. I am Strong and Smart." He said while passing my wine glass in my hand. *"Cheers to two equal people,"*

"Cheers to friendship and love." She spoke.

Those words, rang a bell in my mind. I am sure, that I had heard the exact same line by someone else. But I could not remember by whom and when.

My mind reminded me of the agenda that I had come here for: I could tick mark as done to only the window view being checked. How could I know where she keeps her bunch of keys of the beach bungalow? No way, could I ask her directly about it.

"Martha, did you buy all of these savouries from a restaurant? I say so because they are so extremely perfect to look at and so amazing to taste too." There was a dejected look on Martha's face. *"I am not taking that as an insult, but rather as a compliment."*

Two out of the three agendas on my list were attended to. The third and last one was the most difficult one. I cannot leave till I get a scanned copy of the beach bungalow keys.

"Martha, I am a down to the earth person. I like to sit or squat on the floor and have my drinks. Is it okay with you?

"Absolutely not," said Martha. *"Feel free. Make yourself comfortable. I too will join you with my glass and bring the tray of snacks to the floor."*

The ground of Martha's room was not bare tiled flooring. It had a rich and thick carpet spread from edge to edge of the entire room. It was so dense and thick that it had a certain amount of cushioning effect to it. When I squatted on the floor, I felt my big hard butts like resting on soft pillows.

By now as we squatted comfortably on the floor, this was our third round of wine pegs from the bottle. I could see the bottle still half empty. I binged on the snacks, like there is no tomorrow. Martha got up and refilled the snack tray. With a strict motherly sounding tone, she said,

"No more for you. You have to keep space for my food and your ice cream desert too."

I had to admit to Martha, that rest of the three snacks I have had earlier. But the fried bread fruit was so crispy and had a very unique and exotic taste.

Martha's phone call was buzzing and ringing with a call. From the tone of it, seemed to be an international call. And it was. Martha attended to the call. It was her daughter Jennifer's video call from Croatia.

Suddenly Martha turned her Phone camera on me, so that her daughter could see her mother's friend. Jennifer had just seen the Ice Cream Birthday cake song video shared by her mother to her. Jennifer was very happy, that her mother was celebrating her birthday in Goa.

Martha said: *"My daughter said that you are a very handsome man. She said that she was glad that I was not alone today, and was celebrating her daughter's birthday with someone. She told me to Enjoy."*

"I hope you are enjoying," Suman inquired.

"Suman, you have made my daughter very happy and so indeed you have made me very happy too. Ask me for anything that you want."

I kept quiet.

Martha's western skirt was a bit tight; she was a bit uncomfortable sitting on the floor.

So as to comfortably squat in yoga position on the floor, she with her two cooks' strong hands, ripped the right side of her skirt. This gave ample of room for her healthy legs to squat properly.

Now Martha sat comfortably in a crossed legged pattern. This made her skirt to naturally roll quite a bit higher, thus exposing her inner white legs and thighs.

She was amply drunk on wine by now, for it to matter to her. Comfort was more important than being modest at all times.

With three glasses of wine down my tummy and not to forget the earlier four Kingfisher beers, I was naturally getting aroused seeing her sexy inner thighs.

I made another peg of wine for the two of us. Clinging our glasses together, *"Cheers. Said Martha. To new friendships and love."*

This time she used the word, *"New"*. It added a certain kind of freshness to the same toast.

We continued sipping on the wine and gobbling on the snacks. We chatted on this and that. We laughed at each other's silly jokes.

With the wine bottle totally empty, Martha suggested that we should both eat as the wine made her hungry. She was right. Wine is an appetiser and it makes you hungry for more better and finer things in life.

She requested me to set the table outside on the terrace under the starry lit sky. I too agreed with that. With wobbly feet Martha too started to bringing the food to the table. Last she brought a candle lit lamp.

When Martha went into the room to get some cutlery, my head twisted towards the approaching mud road that comes towards the Kumar's bungalow.

From this height, I could clearly see the silhouette of a sufficiently broad-shouldered man slowly yet casually walking towards Kumar's bungalow.

It was like me seeing me, in some time travel movie. Only this was not me. I was on the guest house terrace with Martha.

The stranger climbed on to the veranda. Just like I had done, he removes his shoes, ties his shoe laces together and then hangs them around his neck.

This was like some fucking dejavu happening to me. I stood there transfixed trying to understand what was happening.

Then I heard Martha come and stand beside me. She too started looking towards the Kumar's bungalow. I told her what I had seen. She remarked, *"Ignore it. It's just one of many Sachaladevi's lovers."*

Ignore it. *It's just one of many Sachaladevi's lovers.*

This could mean, that the first night I came to Sachaladevi's house, Martha surely saw me. But maybe she could recognise that it was me. I hoped it was so.

With that thought, I started eating at the vast spread of food on the folding table on the terrace. This was food fit for the Gods. Hot food daily and a hot woman on the bed, then what made Martha's husband an alcoholic, I just could not understand and figure that out.

As Martha was eating her food with her hands, I got up in the middle of my dinner. I said to her. Sorry I am a little drunk. But this is my best way of complimenting to the world's best cook.

I took her gravy filled hand, turned her palm and graciously kissed the backside of her palms. Then I proceeded to lick the delicious, *"Butter Chicken"* gravy directly from each of her long fingers. Licking each one slowly, sexily and seductively.

I moved behind her wooden folding chair, moved her chin upwards towards me and kissed her on the lips.

She put in some effort to open her mouth to say, *"There is no butter chicken there."*. I did not stop kissing on her comment. Slowly she let loose herself and opened her mouth fully to my kisses. I was now French kissing her deep in the gorges of her mouth." I took a break to comment. *"There's lots of butter chicken here."*

This was so true. As she had just eaten a good portion of her own cooked butter chicken. I moved my two hands over her silky dress and two breasts. She urged me to stop. *"Not here. Not here."* She pleaded.

I gave in to her request. *"Let me shower first, otherwise you will get to eat all the same food smells from my body."* That surely made perfect sense to me too. She carried all the leftover food to the kitchen and made me do the same.

Leave the other things on the table as it is. Cleaning staff will attend to it tomorrow. So, no worries. Come in and make yourself comfortable on the bed. I will shower fast and come soon.

I undressed myself and made myself comfortable in her large Queen size bed. Waiting for her impatiently.

While going for her shower, she puts off all the lights in the main room. But the moonlight hitting from outside created enough play of light and shadows to brighten the room. In another ten minutes or so, I hear the shower being turned off. And there she emerges at the entrance of the room.

She was wearing the same blue night gown that Sachaladevi wore on the night that we made ecstatic love on the terrace and the water tank.

♥

Chapter 7

The Portuguese Chapel.

I forgot to mention, how I completed my third agenda on visit list to Martha's room.

After a frantic bout of lovemaking with Martha, two things happened that are worth recollecting and telling:

Firstly, since we both were drunk, we were fumbling and bumbling in bed. All throughout the love making session, I could only see Sachaladevi's face on Martha's body. I think it was due to the same nightgown of Mrs. Kumar.

Secondly, something very uncanny and eerie happened while I had penetrated Martha, in my drunken stupor I took Sachaladevi's name a couple of times while rhythmically going in and out in the well lubricated vagina by now.

The drunk Martha too called out a name. No. Not mine. Twice, during our love session, she spoke the name, "Babu, Babu". Who the fuck was Babu? Maybe it was Baby she was calling out to me lovingly. I let that thought get lost there.

Now it totally and thoroughly dawned upon me, that the Maid Martha knew about my affair with her Madam Sachaladevi.

Martha being a full time and permanent inhouse maid had complete trust and access to all the areas of the Kumar's beach bungalow, so it must have not been difficult for Martha to pick up the same blue Nightgown that Mrs. Sachaladevi was wearing on our rendezvous night.

***"Martha just did not have a copy of the key to Kumar's bungalow.** She rather was the key to the bungalow."*

Late in the middle of the night, after having separated myself from Martha's embrace, I tip toed out of bed, still completely stark naked. I started frantically looking around this living room cum kitchen studio room of the Maid Martha. For an extra beam of light, I put my phone torch light on. I found a key hanger on the wall. There was a big fat bunch of keys hanging. I had seen them last night, while Martha was opening the main guest house door. So, it was not these. The other tinier bunch of bungalow keys just could not be found.

After few minutes of looking and searching around, Martha's voice broke the deafening silence in her room.

"Sir Suman". The Sir title came back again. *"Are you looking for these"?* There in her hands, was a tiny and shiny bunch of keys, the stainless steel of the keys shining in my phone torch light.

I was totally tongue tied and looked like a thief who was caught red handed while trying to steal something.

"Take them. Do whatever you want to do with them."

"All you had to do, was ask me for them", I would have given them to you. Stupid Suman. When a woman gives her body to you, she gives everything to you."

"But get these back to me in the same order, tomorrow on Sunday anytime."

"I have to report to duty at the bungalow only on Monday morning."

Having said that, she pulled the bedspread and rolled her naked body gently in, back to sleep.

Within seconds, as though I was not existing, I could hear Martha gently slipping into deep sleep as a baby and was snoring like a baby elephant.

I could not believe my luck. I safely tucked in the Kumar bungalow keys into deep denim jeans pocket.

I exited the guest house. Then enjoyed the walk which was now a decline towards the property boundary wall. I noticed a two-way night latch lock on the door. This got me worried. Did I forget to ask Martha about this access key.

Instinctively my hand reached into my pants pocket and pulled out bunch of keys given by Martha. I started comparing the keys with the look of the lock on the door. After a few failed tries, I achieved success. Martha had thought about this in advance. She was thoughtful and kind.

Pushing the boundary door to get automatically locked, I continued walking steadily downhill. I was now passing by the old Portuguese chapel. It was as if time had stood still somehow here, with this monument being a silent spectator to all of the sins of different generations of people long gone. If only stones, could talk I thought, this Portuguese Chapel would have lots of interesting stories to tell.

With that thought in mind, I moved on. The chapel was now above me, in the near distance. I pressed on myself start button and the bullet bike purred like one big cat back to life.

I reminded myself, that I had to return the Bungalow keys tomorrow max by evening, back to Martha in time, otherwise it will land her in unnecessary trouble, because of stupid me.

Having reached home to my Pollem beach house, shat, showered and slumped my tired body on my soft bed. The last thought before I was fast asleep was, *"Who the fuck is Babu"?*

I woke up to a bright and sunny Sunday morning. Another day and another set of new worries. SET. Oh shit, I suddenly remembered. I have to make an urgent copy of the whole set of the Kumar's bungalow keys.

I remember I had safely stored the number of a professional key maker in Margao city. I just remembered by heart the following:

AKSHAY KEY MAKER

Old Station Road

I found the saved entry in my personal diary. It was Akshay Key Maker, Old Station Road, Sanskar Society, Margao.

His phone number too was saved in the name of Akshay Key Maker.

Being Sunday and shops being closed everywhere in Goa, I had difficulty in convincing him to open shop only for me. He made me agree, that he will be charging double of his normal standard rates for this special service. He seemed eager to come soon when I communicated to him that I needed copies made for around 12 + keys or more. The opportunity to earn something more, ensured him coming and opening shop for me.

As promised over the phone, Akshay arrives much before his stated time of 11 am, that Sunday morning.

I had earlier done many copies of keys from Akshay. I knew him for the past decade and never had I too come twice for any key not opening the lock in the very first try. He used to make key copies by an automated engraving machine that cost a million or little more. At the very first output the machine used to give a perfect same to same copy of the original. Akshay was sort of a perfectionist when it came to keys. He even used the same metal as in the original key.

He had ready to use metal blocks in brass, copper, bronze, alloy, aluminium and many more.

By early 4 pm, all of Kumar bungalow keys were ready. Akshay insisted on putting a separate keychain for the new copies to identify easily which one is original and which one was the copied set.

Again, I remembered that Martha and myself, we both had forgotten to ask each other our phone numbers. There was no way of intimating her of my arrival. But I remember her telling me that I can come, anytime on Sunday.

I wondered what if I bumped into Sachala on the way to the guest house, what do I say? My mind persuaded me to understand, that a Celebrity like Sachala wont physically stress herself in the open Goan hot sun walking uphill and downhill just to meet Martha. She could beckon the maid with one simple call.

I reached the Kumar's guest house a little before 06 pm, evening time. Now in broad daylight, I could see a modern intercom Video phone integrated in the laterite stone wall besides the wooden door. I pressed the GO LIVE button and kept it depressed. Within seconds, Martha was on the screen.

After exchanging greetings and pleasantries, she instructed me to kindly leave the keys in the Red Post Box on the side wall marked as *"Martha"* in her name. I will collect it a little later. She thanked me for delivering it back on time.

I gently slided the bunch of keys in the red box marked with her name. There a few other more postal boxes there too. On dropping the keys, there was not metal falling on metal sound, that I expected. It meant, that there was some previous postal material that was not collected or cleared from her box.

I decided to spend some quality time, around the Portuguese Chapel as I had the entire evening free from work and other appointments.

Today in the bright twilight light, as the sun was setting, but the skies were bright and blue, I could appreciate the beauty of this ancient structure more closely and clearly.

I wished I could enter it and explore it more closely. Then I notice a small intrepid black lock that was less black and more rusted brown in color. It told me that very rarely this lock was being opened.

A thought entered my mind. An eerie wishful thought. Could the bunch of Kumar's Beach Bungalow keys have this Chapel key too. My heart started racing like that of a teenage boy, Jack who was the character and member of the Secret Seven gang, an epic novel by Enid Blyton.

I systematically tried one key at a time. Only one key was even able to enter the keyhole of this lock. All others were immensely huge. I inserted the tiny key into this chapel lock. Twisted it once clockwise. It turned. But the lock did not open. I could not pull the key out too. It seemed as it was stuck. Then it dawned upon me.

Old ancient locks needed to be twisted or turned twice. With a firm grip and turned the key in the same clock wise direction again. And there was the "tuck" sound of the lock handle thrown loose and open. Wow. What a luck.

I pushed open the Iron Rods tall horizontal twin doors ajar and entered inside. I got a deep nauseating smell of dampness. Of a place not visited and maintained regularly. I was about to enter further in, when I realized it's better to close the lock from the inside, that way no one, not even Martha from top, or any passerby will know that someone has entered inside, that too without permission.

The chapel had three altars with the middle one little bigger than the ones besides it. The main altar had at its center a life size statue of Mother Mary, with the inscribed words in stone, *"Our Lady of the Mount"*. Mother Mary as always was holding the baby Jesus in her endearing arms. Above it was a picture of some gold crown coronation over some female's head.

I believe it must be the same Virgin Mary before she became mother of Jesus. At the base of this altar were two statues one of St. Vincent with a ship and St. Lawrence.

I dusted one of the few wooden pews there and sat in deep meditation. I realized that the world always was in need of heroes and heroines in all cultures and faiths. The world needs the high standard values and moral woman, like Mother Mary. Virginity was no longer safeguarded and treasured for the marriage bed. Every female from every community was eager to lose her virginity, much before her marriage night. That's why the world needed a Virgin Mother Mary.

I got bored staring at the ancient altar and was about to stand up and leave. That very time, I heard the sound something small crashing on the floor at some distance.

I totally got spooked and scared. I was inside some ancient chapel, that too without anybody's permission.

If I was detected, then it would be a serious matter of Trespassing in private property, plus I would be caught with a copy of the chapel key and bungalow keys. Not only trespassing, this was a serious matter of breaking into someone's property. To make matters worse, this was a religious Christian monument and I was a Hindu. I decided that I have to leave in haste.

If I locked myself from the inside. For others to not know my illegal presence, Then the other person, whoever it was had also ensured to lock themselves from the inside. Whoever it was, was moving around secretly, just like me.

Without wasting much time, I got myself out of the chapel within few seconds and was twisting the lock for the second time from outside the chapel. Now it was pitch dark outside and I was sure if Martha was standing at her window, she would not be either able to see or recognise me.

As I was turning my back to the chapel, I saw a faint movement of a human figure near the altar chapel. All I could assume that it was a man. The only thing that caught the attention of my eyes was, the simple and cheap white canvas shoes that I used to wear during my school days. Oh my God, I thought. Hope that was not a ghost or spirit of someone from decades ago. The canvas shoes were from that old generation.

Out of fear and urgency of not catching anyone's attention I ran swiftly towards my Bullet Bike safely parked and ambushed in the mangrove bushes. My bullet bike had a military green paint color, so it always got easily camouflaged in any natural green background.

While riding my bullet bike back to Pollem, the white canvas shoes was going round and round in my mind.

"Who wears white canvas shoes in this modern age and time?"

♥

Chapter 8

Debacle in Sharjah

Early Monday morning, I was awakened by the constant ringing of my mobile phone. Before taking the call, had a glance at my wristwatch. The digital time will be etched in my memory forever.

03:33 AM

25th February 2024

Who at this unearthly hour, in the middle of the night and morning dared to make this call and disturb my sleep.

It was an unknown call from an unknown number. I had never ever received a call ever before from this phone number.

I decided to ignore the call. Must be a wrong number I guessed and went back to sleep.

Once again, my phone started ringing. The same number kept flashing on my mobile screen. This better not be a wrong number, otherwise I will.... Before I could complete my line of thought, I selected to take the call on my smart phone.

The person on the other end was crying profusely and immensely.

It was the deep cry of a woman who wanted to speak but words were not coming from her mouth.... then I heard the first few words that made me drop my phone from my hand.

"Madam Sachaladevi is no more. Mrs. Sachaladevi is dead."

My whole body was trembling. I lay in a frozen, but trembling manner in my bed, with the caller's words creating sort of an echoing effect in my brains. I could not stop the words playing and repeating on its own again and again in my brains. "Madam, Sachaladevi is no more. Mrs. Sachaladevi is dead."

I did not need to ask, who the caller was. I recognized her voice. Somehow, she managed to locate and find my phone number from somewhere. It was Martha the Maid.

I got out of my bed and switched the TV on. This idiot box was rarely switched on in these days of Internet. By default, my first opening channel was HBO the movie channel. I located the remote and pressed on the NEWS blue button on my remote. This facility showed a PIP (Picture in Picture) feature of around 12 + channels but without any news channel audio on.

All the 12 PIP blocks were featuring some photo or video of Mrs. Sachaladevi. I switched to BBC to hear the news as my first choice. The news readers ominous and sad sounding voice broke my heart. *"Bollywood Celebrity and Star of Hindi Cinema is dead. I repeat again. Mrs. Sachaladevi Kumar is dead."* She was reading and repeating her news script as though she was confirming to herself that Sachaladevi is dead.

I went to my smart phone back once again. My message notifications at night time were always kept muted and in silent mode. There were hundreds of messages and news video links sent by one and all to my what's app message inbox.

My entire world around me seemed to be collapsing. I had to run to the commode and bend down on my two feet as I profusely vomited out my guts empty. Last night's eaten food, half-digested was out through my mouth and into the commode.

Once I stopped puking, then I noticed the start of a splitting headache. I rushed to my medicine cabinet and flushed down two tablets of Crocin 650 Paracetamol painkillers.

The pain in my brain, Crocin would kill, being a pain killer. The aching pain and gaping hole in my heart would remain forever and would end in death only.

The shock of Sachaladevi being no more was slowly but surely sinking in.

Internet News Clip

The Sharjah Public Prosecutors Office has closed the investigation into Bollywood actor Mrs. Sachaladevi Kumar's death and cited the forensic report to say she had accidentally drowned following loss of consciousness.

♥

Chapter 9

Accidental Drowning

Having studied myself from reputed international universities, I was wary about the wrong choice of words in English as used by the Sharjah Public Prosecutors office. I wondered if the legal law system functioned in English language or Arabic.

How can any educated and sane person use the word accidental before the word of drowning, which by itself its meaning is "accidental incident".

It's like the Sharjah Government are saying Sachaladevi's death was due to an ACCIDENTAL ACCIDENT.

Then I thought to myself: If one can call, whatever happened on the last fateful dying day of Sachaladevi as accidental drowning. Then I accidentally fucked Martha. The maid slipped on a banana skin peel and she accidentally fell on my hard erect penis.

I continued thinking of similar crazy situations:

Accidental Marriage

Accidental Murder

Accidental Suicide

Accidental Robbery

Accidental Plane Crash and so many more.

I was not the only one thinking in this original direction. Any educated and intelligent mind would think in a similar fashion.

The entire fan community was abuzz with the same thought. Too say, this topic became viral on the internet among all the STUPID IDIOTS.

Dictionary meaning of drowning:

Drowning is death caused by being underwater and unable to breathe. A drowning is a death that happens in this way.

There have been a few drownings over the years.

A verdict of accidental death by drowning was recorded.

Collins Dictionary.

Even Collins dictionary accurately used the word accidental along with the word death.

Sharjah Public Prosecutors job was to identify the immediate cause of death and not try to convince that there was no foul play or illegal intent or criminal motive of any kind.

By the Public prosecutor admitting that it was an "Accidental drowning", it's like he re-enforcing the thought and idea, that it was not drowning by Intention. Intention that is of a third party or of someone else intending to kill or murder Sachaladevi.

It was like saying that one's own body became an "Anti-body" and was thus "Anti life" and the body slipped by itself into two feet of Bath tub water and remained in reclining sleeping mode till it got drowned by itself. WOW

Here is what Google's AI has to say on "Accidental Drowning":

Accidental drowning occurs when someone dies by submerging in water and their respiratory system is cut off from oxygen.

It can be caused by a number of factors, including:

Lack of swimming skills

Inadequate supervision

Failure to take precautions

Hazardous conditions in or around the water

Alcohol consumption

Birth defects

Drowning is a leading cause of accidental death globally, accounting for 7% of all injury-related deaths. Children, males, and people with increased access to water are most at risk.

My mind started racing and pacing and trying to find answers regarding accidental drowning and the possibility and probabilities of such an accident happening.

If drowning is an accident by itself, then how can one have an accidental drowning situation?

First, we need to Understand Accidental Drowning Situations:

To answer the question of how drowning can be considered as an accident while also probing the possibility of an "accidental drowning situation," one must first make clear the definitions and contexts involved.

Definition of Drowning

Drowning is defined by the World Health Organization (WHO) as the process of experiencing respiratory loss from submersion or immersion in any liquid, including water.

This lack of respiratory functions of the humans' lungs, due to loss of oxygen, happens only when one's head is fully submerged under water.

This lack or loss of sufficient oxygen for life, can result in death, morbidity, physical damage and permanent injury to the body or brain.

The main point, here is that drowning happens when a person is unable to breathe due to being submerged in any liquid or water, which can happen in various environments such as pools, lakes, oceans, and even bathtubs.

Accidents and their generality in nature.

An accident is classically understood as an unintentional, unintended and unplanned event that results in bodily harm, injury and even death many a times.

In this context, "accidental drowning" refers to situations where individuals unintentionally find themselves in circumstances leading to drowning.

This implies that while drowning itself is a specific outcome (the event of suffocating or being submerged under water), the events leading up to it can be classified as accidents.

Accidental Drowning Explained

An accidental drowning refers precisely to occurrences where a person drowns unintentionally and involuntarily.

If drowning is done by self, by the person himself or herself, then it is drowning by suicide.

If drowning is done by force, by another individual or multiple persons in ensuring that the drowning person is forcibly and violently kept submerged under water till he or she dies, then it is a homicide or drowning by murder.

If drowning happens just by chance, meaning that the individual person had absolutely no intention of getting drowned; but it was a consequence of unforeseen circumstances, incidents or accidents then it is called accidental drowning.

Few Examples of possible accidental drowning scenarios:

Inadequate Supervision: A child may slip into a pool while playing without adult supervision.

Medical Emergencies: An adult may suffer a heart attack while swimming and subsequently drown.

Environmental Factors: Strong currents in a river may sweep away a swimmer who underestimated the water conditions.

Accidental Drowning Situations

The term "accidental drowning situation" encompasses scenarios where various factors contribute to an unintentional drowning event. These situations often involve:

Lack of Safety Measures: Absence of life jackets, pool barriers, or lifeguards increases the risk.

Human Error: Misjudgement regarding about one's own swimming abilities or lack of knowledge about environmental hazards can lead to accidents.

Alcohol Consumption: Impairment of our brains motor functions, and reflexes due to high alcohol consumption can significantly increase the possibility and probability of drowning incidents to happen.

How Accidental Drowning mostly Occurs

Unforeseen Circumstances: Many accidental drownings happen due to unforeseen circumstances. For example, a person may slip and fall into a body of water suddenly without any warning. This slip constitutes an accident because it was not planned or intended. Or in other more simpler words, the person was in the wrong place and at the wrong time.

Lack of Supervision: In many cases, particularly involving children, accidental drownings happen when there is unsatisfactory or absolutely no adult supervision. A child may wander and meander away from their parents, guardians, or caretakers and fall into a pool, lake or water body without anyone noticing until it's too late.

Inexperience or Lack of Skills: Human beings, who are not natural, strong or professional swimmers may misjudge and miscalculate their personal abilities and venture into deeper unsafe waters than they are capable to handle.

Especially in strong currents scenarios in rivers and seas, when they struggle and cannot keep their heads afloat above water, for regular intake of oxygen via mouth or nostrils, then this scenario leads to accidental drowning.

Environmental Factors: Climatic and environmental Conditions can change suddenly without much warnings, such as strong currents, waves, or sudden weather changes can create dangerous situations for swimmers, kayakers, or people indulging in water sport activities, who may not be prepared for such sudden challenges.

Alcohol Consumption: Alcohol relaxes the nerves in the brains and weakens our judgment and reduces our physical coordination, and motor skills, which can lead people to participate in risky behaviours around water bodies, which could ultimately result in accidental drownings.

Medical Emergencies: Sometimes individuals may suffer sudden medical emergencies like heart attacks or asthma attack or epileptic attack, while swimming or boating, leading them to lose consciousness and subsequently drown.

Conclusion on Accidental Drowning

Drowning in any water body, including the least water in a bath tub too can lead to respiratory failure.

An "accidental drowning situation" refers exactly and explicitly to the conditions and contributing factors that leads to this unintended, unplanned and unexpected result.

To summarize briefly, all accidental drownings are indeed accidents; however, they occur within specific situations characterized by negligence, environmental hazards, or unforeseen medical issues. Also, accidental drowning situations arise from various risk factors and human behaviours that culminate in unintentional drownings.

♥

Chapter 10

Death never pays. Insurance does.

Time and Tides of the Oceans wait for no one. Time has been always ticking ahead. The oceans hitting their tides incessantly on every beach shore. Change is said to be the only constant in life. Change has, was, is and will be always happening. Just like time, change is every changing itself with the times and tides of life.

If change is constant, then death is a permanent fact of life. Nothing really lasts forever. Not life. Not love. Not lust. Nothing. We humans are just visiting tourists on planet earth.

Humankind has spent millions if not billions on research and development, but medical science has not been able to beat or destroy death.

Even Jesus Christ, one of the few people who claimed to have got resurrected and overcame death did not prove it to be a fact because all of those that overcame death, they did for their personal self and glory. None of them passed on that knowledge of beating or overcoming death, while living forever on earth immortally. All were selfish. They resurrected themselves and disappeared their own self, where the Creator of this universe only knows.

Death does not pay. Hence in an eventuality of dying under certain specified conditions and carriers, then Insurance companies pay. Multiple reports started flooding the internet, that Sachaladevi had an insurance policy worth ₹240 crore in Oman, which could only be claimed if she died in Sharjah.

The death of the actress, who drowned in a bathtub in a Sharjah hotel, was initially reported as an accidental drowning. However, some speculated that her death was a planned murder, and that the insurance policy was a factor.

Details surrounding the insurance policy & Sachaladevi's death

Insurance policy: Some local Indian lawyer, claimed that Sachaladevi had an insurance policy in UAE that could only be claimed if she had an accident while working or living in UAE or have died in Sharjah.

Indian Supreme Court rejection: The Supreme Court rejected a petition for India to do its independent investigation and thus challenge the forensic decision of the UAE Government. This would have a geo-political conflagration and would stain the extremely good foreign relations and trade between the two friendly countries.

Sharjah Police: Initial reports released by The Sharjah Police said that Sachaladevi died after losing consciousness, due to High BP and over consumption of alcohol at last nights wedding party.

Close Relatives Report: Most of the close relatives of Mrs. Sachaladevi repeatedly reported that they were informed that Sachaladevi had died from a major Cardiac arrest – a major Heart attack.

Post-mortem report: The official post-mortem report stated that Sachaladevi died from accidental drowning.

Delay in returning remains: There were delays in returning Sachaladevi's remains to India, which led to speculation about the cause of her death.

Forensic experts' investigation: Forensic experts claimed that Sachaladevi should have fallen flat on her back if her death was an accident, but she was found face down in the tub. They suggested that it appeared the drowning was forced in the bath tub by one or more persons.

NOTE: A mummified body was presented to India, without any internal organs.

♥

Chapter 11

Time heals wounds or Time buries wounds.

There is a common saying since centuries, that time heals all wounds. But I feel that time hides or buries our wounds.

The hurt, the pain, the anger, the resentment all of those hurtful and hateful feelings get resurrected if time scratches deep enough. Hate does not hurt the dead. Hate hurts the living. Hate can hurt and handicap someone for life. Higher the hate, it can even kill.

After the last condolence visit to Sir Bharat Kumar's residence, I happened to be briefly introduced to both of his daughters who were studying in some far away foreign country.

Bollywood celebrities tend to make their diamonds from the vernacular Hindi movie industry, but I found them, majority, can almost saw all of them always speaking in the English language only at all of their official movie launches, mahurats, parties, business meetings and even on the Hindi movie sets. The Hindi movie director always gives the directions and instructions in English to all of the artists and performers. When angry, they curse in Hindi.

All the Bollywood stars avoid speaking Hindi by heart, at home or anywhere at all. The only time the Bollywood stars speak Hindi is while working to make and remove money from their billions of Indian Hindi fans. Hindi is treated like a Harijan language, fit to be spoken only by the mass poor and middle-class Indians. Our money is not untouchable.

Our language and country are for these new English speaking Goras of our very own country, like some third-class train compartment which by itself does not exist.

So, to find the Kumar's two daughters studying and living abroad was not shocking to me at all.

Bollywood speaks English, walks English, shits on English commodes, fucks English Missionary style, study in English universities and live like English Goras in some far away foreign country. Sachaladevi was a true Tamilian and Indian at heart. Her first home was Chennai and second home was Goa.

At the last condolence meeting at the Kumar's beach bungalow, I happened to feel and find, Martha looking different. She was no longer wearing the official uniform of a Maid.

I remember as a professional Nanny, it was Martha who was always raising the two girls from infancy to their adulthood. She was the one who smothered them both with lots of love, while the Mother Sachaladevi was busy as an actress on filmy reels making money and also an actress in real life.

The two daughters seemed to have got over the death of their biological mother, as they never missed her in death, because she was always missing at home, away out on work from them. Since Sachaladevi's death, I found that Martha the maid had totally disappeared into oblivion. Only few people knew about Martha's past. I was one of the few last.

The two children were lovingly calling Martha as Martha Amma or it was like she was christened with a new Tamilian name, Marthama. What a transformation I was seeing right in front of my eyes. Martha who was the Maid by day and a Nun by night, today was Mother Martha.

Something was straight amiss in this new family scene. My eyes seemed to be going again and again to the life size portrait photo of Sachaladevi hanging graciously on the main living room wall and coincidentally both her daughters were sitting on a large sofa just below this wall hanging. The eldest daughter Janaki was looking so similar to her mother Sachaladevi. I thought the younger daughter had not got any features from her mother, but she looked more like her father Bharat Kumar. As this thought was going through my mind, with the sound of hundreds of guests coming in with their condolences.

Everyone wanted a selfie shot with the new Kumar family. Someone called out loud: *Jennifer, can you please come for one family click with us".* I turned around to see and realize that Jennifer was the name of the second daughter of Bharat Kumar, whose name I did not know. I only knew of Janaki.

At the sound of Jennifer's name being called out, two people's heads cocked and turned 360 % simultaneously and at the same time, staring deeply into each other's eyes. This just cannot be happening. This was just too shocking even for me to digest. The soft drink glass slipped from my hand as I lost my balance. I knew I was fainting. As I fell down with a thud, somebody seemed to scream and tell to call for an ambulance, Pandeyji has fainted and collapsed. As I was slowly drowning deeper and deeper into unconsciousness, the last conversation that I heard around me was that of Sir Bharat Kumar asking Martha, what happened to Pandeyji. Martha replied, *"Babu, Pandeyji fainted out of exertion." "He needs to be urgently taken to some hospital".*

***"Babu,** Pandeyji fainted out of exertion." "He needs to be urgently taken to some hospital".*

♥

Chapter 12

Everything that has a beginning has to have an End.

I love watching the old Tetralogy of the four, "Matrix" movies.

Matrix has multiple meanings, including a mathematical concept, a term used in geology, and a science fiction film franchise:

The Matrix is a science fiction film franchise that includes the following films:

The Matrix (1999)

The Matrix Reloaded (2003)

The Matrix Revolutions (2003)

The Matrix Resurrections (2021)

Very few movie lovers know that the word Matrix has another ancient and deeper meaning connected to the Jewish bible.

The word, "Matrix" appears 5 times in the KJV English translation of the Jewish bible. Always it appears with the phrase, "all that openeth the Matrix"

Matrix is an English translation of the Hebrew word, "Rechem", meaning Womb.

And openeth, is meaning that which first opens. So the phrase means that which first opens the womb. In other words, the mother's firstborn.

The English word, "Matrix" comes from the same word in Latin, meaning, Womb. Which in turn comes from MATER, meaning MOTHER.

At the time of translation of the Hebrew bible into English language, matrix meant womb in the English language. But with passage of time, Matrix has taken on different meanings biology, mathematics, electronics and computing.

It is because of these multiple meanings as well of its use in the Bible that the WACHOWSKIS chose it as a name for their 1999 movie. The Matrix. The matrix is both a computer simulation for the human minds and a machine womb for their bodies.

The line *"Everything that has a beginning has an end" is* spoken by The Oracle in the 2003 movie The Matrix Revolutions: *"Everything that has a beginning has an end. I see the end coming, I see the darkness spreading. I see death"*

A few four years had passed since the death of my beloved Sachala, devi to the world, most dear to me.

Not a single day passed without thinking of Sachala. Not a single day ended without wishing, hoping and praying for justice for her.

Four years later, I was travelling alone from Mumbai to Israel via a stopover at Abu Dhabi airport. While relaxing and sipping some local GAVAH (bitter Arabic coffee), I happened to be watching the local news channel of Qatar's Al Jazeera, I was staring at an old profile picture of Sachaladevi on TV.

I rushed to the coffee counter and requested to increase the sound of the TV. The salesboy immediately obliged. I realized that the news reader was speaking in Arabic, which I could not understand anything at all. I asked if anyone could translate to me just the gist of the current news item featuring the late Bollywood star Sachaladevi. A gentleman kindly obliged. I was all ears to him. He started telling me that, the news reader is stating that rumours are floating all over Goa, in India, that Mrs. Sachaladevi has come back. As a Ghost. I asked him why so? He was surprised that I being Indian, did not know. Did not know what?

Sir Bharat Kumar and his newly married wife were both found dead together in their own bath tub.

"How so? How did they both die in the bath tub?"

The gentleman replied, *"According to the Post Mortem and Forensic reports that came. The official reason for death was recorded and reported as: "Accidental Electrocution", while having a bath in the bath tub."*

Four years ago, Mrs. Sachaladevi had died by "Accidental Drowning" in a hotel bath tub in Sharjah. Recently her husband Bharat Kumar and his new wife Martha died in a similar fashion by "Accidental Electrocution". Hence the local gossip in Goa is that Mrs. Sachaladevi has come back to her home at Cavellossim in Goa.

As I sat transfixed looking at Sachala on the tv screen, I heard the last and final boarding announcement for my Abu Dhabi to Israel flight. I was leaving India for good. With this new development, it was good that I was not available for any kind of investigation in India.

No one will believe me. I cannot believe it myself. I totally forgot that I had not disconnected the "killer feature" in the bath tub.

Once my Israel Airlines, flight took off for Tel Aviv, I asked the air hostess if she could fetch me any current International English newspaper for reading. She kindly obliged and provided me the latest issue of "The Al – Khaleej Times."

Half of the front newspaper was dedicated to one single clear colour photograph of Bharat and Martha laying sprawled naked and dead in their bathtub. The headline caption was: *"Dead in the Bath Tub."*

In the extreme corner of the photograph, I could clearly spot two sparkling white canvas large size shoes, kept out before entering the bath tub. This final photo of the canvas shoes completed my puzzle.

"The handicapped and the dead,
need no shoes."

♥

THE END

SYNOPSIS

Everyone at some point or time in their lives, do fall in love. All the characters in this novel too, are always open to love. In the pursuit of career, success, wealth, love always tends to take the lead.

None of the characters in this cinematic reel to real life story, are truly satisfied and content with their current partners in life.

Just as the desire for unlimited and infinite wealth exists in each individual's life, so also is the pursuit of finding "true love". Love is ethereal. Ethereal meaning, extremely delicate and light in a way that seems not to be of this world.

Love exists among humans, but it persists as an alien, out of this world experience. Lust does not lag much behind, every love or loving experience of the novel characters. It is lurking exactly behind love, like a stealthy leopard cat, coiling to spring on its lovers.

This novel takes you on an adventurous journey of Bollywood producer Mr. Bharat Kumar, his beloved wife, Actress Mrs. Sachaladevi and the bachelor for life and love, Mr. Suman Pandey and not to forget the heavenly maid, Martha.

The quartet of the four, make a very dangerous and tumultuous sort of Bermuda triangle of life, love, lust and their romantic misadventures.

Through this murder mystery, the author makes every turning page to splash on you as a churning wave with fresh passion, lust and lots of loving.

"Murderously Yours" is part of the book series titled, "Live, Love, Lust, Let's go."

www.ingramcontent.com/pod-product-compliance
Ingram Content Group UK Ltd.
Pitfield, Milton Keynes, MK11 3LW, UK
UKHW041352190726
13845UKWH00026B/555

9 789334 141467